Escape from Mondo Tiki Island:
A Two-Fisted South Seas Adventure

John L. Sheppard

First Printing: 2015

ISBN-10:1942086059
ISBN-13:978-1-942086-05-5

PL-117

Paragraph Line Books
Oakland, California

www.paragraphline.com

www.johnlsheppard.com

DEDICATION

For Nancy... always

Also By John L. Sheppard

I ain't afraid to love a man. I ain't afraid to shoot him either.

—Annie Oakley

At Sea!

Maybe I should have jumped ship the moment I saw the mystery box come aboard. The massive wooden crate—labeled in drippy, blood-red stencil, "FISH"—was big enough to contain six coffins. The box was surrounded by a contingent of mysterious government types, all black-suited and wearing aviator's glasses, chattering into radio bricks. We hoisted the FISH box aboard and into the cargo hold, and the government types shuffled into the shadows on the dock until we finished uploading the rest of the cargo, most of the rest of it actual canned fish (salmon). We cast off into the blue ocean en route to Australia via the South Pacific passage.

After three years fighting my way across the Pacific as a private soldier in Uncle Sam's employ ten years earlier, I no longer kidded myself about danger and was always alert to it. The feeling I got from those government types made my danger needle twitch all the way to the right of the dial.

I was the third mate onboard the SS *Mother's Mercy*, a C-1 Victory vessel, sold off after the war to the Konrath Lines, who were good enough to give me a regular job.

I'd fallen in love with these ships during the war, having ridden on one to the Philippines. After being wounded near Puerto Princesa, I took a ride on another one of them back stateside. I spent a year recuperating in a hospital in Oakland, suffering from wounds both visible and invisible. It gave me time to study for the merchant marine examination, which I passed handily. I'd always been a quick study, and had completed most of a bachelor's degree on a scholarship from the Rockefeller Foundation at the University of Chicago before joining the Army in a fit of patriotism. I never bothered to complete the degree. By the time I finished recuperating, we'd dropped the bomb on the Japanese and the war was over. With my pawn-shop-bought sextant in hand, I was ready for a mariner's life. A day ashore is a day wasted!

I had no intention of ever going back to Chicago to sit in claustrophobic classes or to work in my old man's butcher shop on the south side. The thought of working around all that blood and gore was horrifying after what I'd seen in the service.

I had some thoughts of making second mate, first mate and maybe captaining my own vessel, but I'd carved a comfortable niche for myself onboard the *Mother's Mercy*.

The Skipper called me on the 1MC to the bridge, and I hustled up the ladder taking two steps at a time. I found him there alone, save for the able-bodied seaman at the helm. The Skipper waved me into the chartroom and shut the watertight door behind us.

"I know you think we're going directly to Sydney, but we're not," the old man said, petting his considerable chin whiskers like it was a purring cat. "We're heading here." He pointed out a spot on the map that contained no land. In fact, there was nothing near that spot for 500 miles in any direction.

"I see," I said, but I didn't. We locked eyes for a moment and the old man let a sly little grin drip across his Santa Claus face. "It has something to do with that goddamned box, doesn't it?"

"You know better than to ask questions like that in a time like this," he said amiably, but with a hint of menace in his voice. "You want to end up testifying in front of a House subcommittee?"

"No, sir," I said quickly.

"Well then," the old man went. "All right. Carry on, Mister Mate."

"Aye, captain."

Artist of Doom!

I opened the watertight door and walked over to the AB steering the ship, and I'll be damned if it wasn't my old partner-in-crime Buzz Pepper. He was a boney little slip of a man with girlish eyes, a combat artist with the Eighth Army in the Pacific before he was wounded and ended up in the same hospital room with me. While I studied, ol' Buzz drew and painted all the horrifying things he'd seen during the war. I couldn't look at his artwork for long, so I took the opportunity to invite him out for a beer or three. My private's pay and combat pay had accumulated in my absence from the civilized world, and I had no reservations about spending it while getting free chow and board in the hospital. It wasn't hard to sneak out.

We rambled all over Oakland and San Francisco together, Mutt and Jeff. I'm six-foot-four and a well-chiseled 210 pounds. Buzz was five-foot-six and probably didn't weigh much more than a buck forty. I have a mop of curly black hair atop my head, an aquiline nose and brownish-black eyes, thanks to my southern Italian heritage. My old man came over from Capua shortly after World War I. Pepper was an unkempt, slouching, prickly little hepcat whose unruly hair twisted this way and that. He hailed from some little burg in Florida, but had no hint of a Southern accent, though he occasionally hinted at having some sort of connection to the circus.

"Pepper, you sly bastard!" I said, slapping him on the back.

He jumped, startled, and looked up and back at me. A smile cascaded across his face. "Russo! How the hell are you!" He stepped back for a moment and surveyed me. "So you really did become an officer in the merchant marine. Khaki looks good on you, mate!"

"Aye, it does," I said, putting my hands on my hips. "And look at you in dungarees!" I said, waving my hand up and down toward him. "When did you start working in the shipping industry?"

"I've been drawing comics for a while, but the industry kind of dried up since the comics code kicked in. I knew a guy who knew a guy and got into the union, and those guys trained me up. And here I am!"

"Damn it's good to see you!"

"And me, you!" We hugged unabashedly, as men who have served together do. After clapping him on the back a time or two, we unembraced. He went back to steering the ship, and I went back to the chartroom to figure out how to chart a course to the middle of nowhere. It would involve a lot of pacing around the room, and coffee. Plenty of that.

Middle Watch!

In the middle of my chartroom peregrinations, the old man dropped in again to check on my progress. "I've put you on middle watch," he informed me in his jolly, yet troubling, manner. He was an old-timer in the shipping biz, predating the merchant marine act by twenty or so years. Wooden ships and iron men. I'd been serving with him for nearly nine years and every time we'd been to sea, he swore it was his last. He claimed to be from New Jersey, yet he didn't sound like an Easterner. He was an anglicized mossback, speaking in a pirate-like squawk, his khakis barely containing his rotund form, and always with a long pipe in hand or mouth, the sweet odor of cherry-scented tobacco wafting off him.

"Middle watch, aye," I said, taking the order like a man. Middle watch, the middle of the night—it was a good time to be awake aboard ship. Just me, the ocean and the stars above and a sextant to guide me. I liked the dark at sea. It was like a soothing cloak. I lit a Chesterfield with my Zippo and felt the tobacco smoke seep into my lungs.

"Mister Mate... Russell..." the captain said, calling me by my first name for the first time in memory. "Make sure you know the way to the rendezvous. Guide us there safely, Mister Mate. All our fates rely on it. Yours most of all."

"Aye, captain... My friends call me 'Russ,'" I tried to think of his first name and failed. "Jimmy?"

He sensed this. "My name's Sullivan. Smilin' Bob Sullivan. My mother called me 'Bob.'"

"Bob," I said, trying it out. It seemed wrong. "Skipper, I won't let you down."

"Make sure you don't, Mr. Mate... er, Russ." He smiled again, a bit wanly. "Make sure you don't. By the way, you can't tell anyone that we're making a stop in the middle of nowhere."

"I'd assumed that, sir."

"You assumed well, mister."

And he left me to my work.

Voyage to Nowhere!

We steamed along at 11 knots for days on end. It would have seemed like a normal ocean crossing if not for the cargo in the hold and the trip to nowhere. And the secrecy. I am not a secrets-type fellow. But since beginning of the War, and the subsequent Cold War, America had become a nation of secrets, of not-loose lips not-sinking ships.

The captain became nervous, and could not sleep. He heard things, and had various twitchings of various appendages informing him of submarines lurking in the cool depths and storms rumbling over the horizon.

Pepper, who volunteered to be the AB steering the ship overnight, was not amused by the captain's constant nervous presence on the bridge. "I volunteered for overnights so I wouldn't have to see the captain. Now I see more of him than I did during the day."

I made coffee, smoked, kept us on course and kept Pepper and the captain company. I took the wheel when Pepper needed to make a head call. The captain sidled up to me and whispered, "He's one of them!"

"One of who?"

"One of them government types! A spook!"

"Ah, hell, Skipper! I know him from my Army days."

"Army, hell! That guy's a spy! My left big toe says so."

"That left big toe has been telling you all sorts of things you should ignore. It told you there was a submarine following us."

"There is!" He took a big puff off his pipe and drummed his belly with the tips of his fingers.

"You should get some sleep, captain," I said, taking another sip of coffee and sucking down the last of a Chesterfield. "Would do you all sorts of good."

"Balderdash! What do you know about the sea! You're from Chicago! You should be navigating iron ore through the Great Lakes, not taking 'fish' halfway to Australia."

"I'll take that under advisement, sir."

"Army! What the hell do you know?"

"I know you need some sleep, sir."

"Old Man Konrath, the owner… you ever meet him?"

"No, sir. Never had the pleasure."

"He's one of them spook-types, too. Sneaky bastard. I think we're carting secret government junk across the ocean in these rigs. You can hide all sorts of goods on a victory ship. They're like a rat maze."

He was right about that. I'd been aboard this ship for years, and yet I often found myself in an unfamiliar spot wondering what the hell was hidden behind an unmarked, waterproof door. There was a compartment amidship labelled "Butcher Shop," and yet I'd never seen fresh meat aboard the vessel, only gravy-soaked chunks ladled out of industrial-sized cans, heated in the galley and served atop reconstituted rice or potatoes. If there was actual fresh meat on board, Charlie Oats, the mate in charge of the galley, was saving it for himself.

"Skipper, you should get some rack time before the forenoon watch. The ship needs your eyes during daylight."

"Aye, she does." And he left.

Pepper peeked inside before entering. "He gone?"

"Yes, it's safe."

Pepper slipped over and took the wheel from me. "He always this nervous?"

"Not generally, no."

"Have something to do with that big box in the hold?"

"I think I'm supposed to say, 'That's classified.'"

Pepper turned and grinned at me. "You don't say?"

"That exotic dancer back in Frisco, what was her name?"

"Eden LaRouche."

"What a name."

"What a body! Hot-cha-cha!"

"She really fell for that line about you being an artist."

"I *am* an artist!"

"That's what makes it a great line!"

"She was a peach."

"A ripe peach."

"An over-ripe peach!" He grinned evilly. "Nice change of subject."

"I thought it was subtle enough."

"Subtle as a two-by-four to the jaw. Where the hell are we going, anyway?"

"Sydney."

"Sydney, eh? I know I'm new to this work, but you wouldn't know we were going to Sydney by the course you're having me steer."

"Don't get yourself into a pickle by asking too many questions. You know, the captain thinks you're with the CIA or something."

"Me? CIA? That's hilarious!" And Pepper forced out a barking laugh that echoed off the rusty bulkheads.

"I'll take that as a 'no.'"

"As I would say in front of a House subcommittee, 'I can neither confirm nor deny...'"

"Ah, a man of mystery."

"That I am, mate! That I am."

"I'm going forward to take a sight." I nipped into the chartroom and picked up my sextant. I emerged and clapped Buzz on the back and smiled at my little friend. "If that's okay with you, Secret Agent Pepper."

He peered at me from the corner of his eye. "Don't get yourself into a pickle, mate."

Sub Spotted!

At night, far out at sea, with no city lights, I could see clearly Libra, Scorpius, Sagittarius and Capricornus twinkling above. I stood on the bow, near where a gun emplacement once was mounted, and breathed in the fresh air, felt the wind in my face, and a great calm washed over me. It was these moments that drew me to the sea, crossing the Pacific that had, only a decade before, been a massive battleground. But at sea, I didn't think such thoughts. At sea, I found my peace.

I took my sights, confirmed that we were on course, and stood for a few more moments there communing with the vast ocean.

I felt a clap on my back and nearly jumped a mile into the air. It was the captain, naturally. "On course, Mister Mate?"

"We are indeed, captain."

"A little jumpy?"

"A bit."

He handed me his binoculars. "Take a look port-side, in the reflection of the moonlight, and tell me what you see."

I peered through the binoculars. "Nothing, sir. Waves."

"Keep looking."

I swept back and forth until I saw it. At first, I couldn't believe my eyes. I magnified and adjusted and saw it very clearly. "A periscope? Is that a periscope?"

"What do you have to say about my left big toe now, mate?"

Commies!

I was fitfully asleep in my cabin when I heard the rap on the door. I'd wrestled my sheets into a bunch. I fell out of my rack, sweating and opened the door to the sight of the first mate, resplendent in a pair of freshly ironed, washed khakis, a blue Dodgers cap on his head. I was dressed in my skivvies and a pair of green, woolen socks. Gil Elvgren was the latest in a long line of first mates we'd had since I'd been aboard. I'd lost count. Elvgren was all business, with a fresh shave on his dimpled chin and Brylcreemed hair. He looked me up and down with disgust. "You're needed on the bridge," he said with a sneer. "Pronto."

"Aye, mate."

"Run a razor across that chin first. Take a little pride, man."

"Aye, sir."

I walked down the p-way to the gang head that the officers shared, shaved and took a sea shower, turning off the taps halfway through and then back on again when I was ready to rinse off. It would be the last shower I'd take for a while.

I reported to the bridge as ordered to find the captain and first mate in a huddle in the chartroom. "Close the door," said the supercilious first.

I did so.

"Have you been tracking the submarine nightly since we first saw it?" the captain asked.

"Aye, sir, that I have."

"It appears only at night, I'm given to understand," the first said.

"Aye, sir. That it does."

"Was it there last night?"

"Aye, captain. Same place we always see it, shadowing us."

"Do we know who it belongs to?" the first asked. "It is ours, or theirs?"

"I don't know, sir."

"Why haven't either of you seen fit to report it to the Navy?"

The captain squinted at the first. "That's my call to make, mister."

"Is it?" the first asked. "I should relieve you of command right now for making that decision."

"I don't think Old Man Konrath would take kindly to that, chum," the Skipper said. He petted his whiskers extra fiercely, like that cat on his chin was going to try to leap off his chest.

The first pressed on like he hadn't heard. "I imagine you two think you're clandestine agents keeping this to yourselves."

"Nothing of the kind, mister," the Skipper said. "Trying not to panic the crew."

"I would think that not being prepared for a commie torpedo would panic the crew more," the first said angrily. "And you! Why exactly are we navigating toward an empty spot in the ocean?"

"I can answer that," the old man said.

"I didn't ask you," the first said.

"Captain's orders," I said.

"That's your defense?"

"That's the truth."

"I ought to punch you in the mouth," the first said.

"Go ahead," I said, feeling the old rage bubbling to the surface. "I'll put your face through that bulkhead."

"Calm down, mates!" the Skipper said. "Or I'll have both of you confined to quarters."

"Shut up, old man!" the first said. "I'm relieving you of command."

The door swung open behind us, and Pepper stepped through it.

"What do you want, seaman?" the first asked.

"Any of you fellas know about a submarine?" Pepper asked.

"Don't listen to the scuttlebutt aboard this bucket," the Skipper said.

"Scuttlebutt, hell!" Pepper said, his girlish eyes twinkling with mischief. "There's a sub off the port bow! Come take a look!"

We ran to the bridge castle front and looked port. Sure enough, there it was, a submarine fully emerged from the depths, a Soviet officer looking at us through a spy glass and a sailor manning a machine gun next to him. They were close enough for us to see the red stars on their caps and the grins on their bleached-white faces. They squinted with their pinprick eyes through the sunlight like a pair of moles. The officer raised a megaphone to his mouth and said, "Dobre den, tovarich! Heave to, and prepare to be boarded!"

"Commies!" the captain exclaimed.

"Heave to? In a pig's eye!" the first said.

"Better do what they say," Pepper suggested, standing behind us. "That machine gun could poke a few holes in this tub, and we're nowhere near land."

"The AB is right," the Skipper said. "We'd better do what they say."

The order was given, dead slow astern, and we slowed to a crawl and then stopped. A team of Soviets climbed into a snoopy boat powered by a sputtering two-stroke and buzzed over, accompanied by the officer, while the sailor on the machine gun kept it leveled at us. "Good morning, captain!" the officer said, once he'd climbed aboard. He smoothed out his uniform, the breast of which was covered over in tinkling medals. A gold belt was cinched around his waist. He shook the captain's hand vigorously while we stood around, amazed at how quickly our fortunes had turned.

"I blame *you* for this," the first said to the captain. "And you, too, third! Some navigator you turned out to be!"

"Quiet, my American friend! There is no need for blame to be given to these gentlemen! They were under orders from the American Navy, were you not?" The rest of his sailors climbed aboard toting AK-47's and a mean attitude, wearing their striped shirts and flat hats adorned with a blood red star, high-waisted black trousers, gritting their tobacco-yellowed teeth. The officer snapped his fingers, and a bottle of vodka made its way into his hand. "But I come bringing a gift. It is, how you say, to wet your whistle. Da?"

"We're not taking your commie vodka!" the first said, taking a step forward.

The sailors didn't hesitate in raising their weapons

from port arms to aiming center mass at the first. "Perhaps you take commie bullet instead?" the officer said. "Ha, ha!"

"Stand fast, first," the Skipper said. He accepted the vodka. "What can we do for you today?"

"We would like some fish," the officer said. "Perhaps you know of special fish that we can have? Hmm?"

"We have plenty of salmon onboard," I said.

"Please not to be, how you say, cute," the officer said, still grinning. "You know what fish we want."

"Aye, we do," the Skipper said dejectedly. "Take them to the hold, mate."

"Your cooperation is appreciated by the Soviet Union," the officer said.

"I'll be goddamned," the first said. And then he punched the officer on the jaw, knocking him backward. The captain, holding the vodka bottle by the neck, flung it end-over-end, and it landed square on the forehead of one of the gun-toting sailors.

This surprised the other sailors who'd accompanied him momentarily, enough time for first and me to jump into action and quickly take them down before they could re-raise their weapons. I heard a shot crack behind me and turned around just after punching my second Soviet cold. It was Pepper, armed with one of the AK-47's, shooting the

Sailor on the machine gun on the Soviet sub. Pepper lowered the rifle after squeezing off his one shot.

"That's some damn fine shooting, AB," the captain said.

"Kentucky windage," Pepper said calmly, like he was talking about picking off a robin from a fence, and not a living human being on a pitching ship at sea from another pitching ship at sea. "Now let's toss these commies overboard and get the hell out of here."

The captain trotted the best he could to the bridge and gave the command for flank speed, while the first, Pepper and I tossed the sailors into the drink and some other AB's pulled their boat aboard.

The first and I double-timed it to the radio room and woke up the radio operator, a whiskey-stinking, toothless slouch in a disheveled half-officer, half-AB uniform. His feet were up next to the radio, his desk chair tilted back to almost falling over, a half-eaten Swiss roll resting on his gut, little brown bits of cake in his blonde-gray beard. "Sparky, wake up!" the first said. "Send out a distress call to Seventh Fleet!"

We knew that the moment the sub submerged, it would be able to outrun us and we'd be dead ducks without some help.

Sparky rubbed the sleep out of his eyes, and shoved

the rest of the roll in his mouth as the first dictated the message. "You sure you want to send the 'SSS' signal?" he asked, spitting out cake. "That means we're under attack by a submarine." He half-dusted off the remains of the cake from his grease-stained and torn chambray shirt.

First gave me a look that said, "What the hell?" and said aloud, "That's exactly what I want to send, you chowderhead! Where the hell have you been?"

"In a cozy slumber," Sparky said, and then he made the call. The radio buzzed and crackled in reply. "Is someone jamming us? Who'd be jamming us this far out at sea?"

"The Russians!" the first and I shouted in unison.

We went back out on the deck. As luck would have it, our ship still had the big eyes from its Navy service, and Pepper had already directed a fellow AB to man them. Other AB's had already appeared, some of them toting the AK-47's left behind by the now-soaked Soviets, and others toting Thompson machine guns. I realized then that I didn't recognize any of the AB's manning the rails.

"Who are these guys?" I asked aloud.

Pepper walked up and slapped me on the back. "Do you really have to ask?"

"Still being paid by Uncle Sugar?"

"You know it, daddy-o."

"Tell me we have back-up," the first said.

"Our backup is the Colt Manufacturing Company," Pepper said, patting his Thompson like a beloved pet. "And a submarine of our own about ten nautical miles behind us. They've been shadowing us the whole time. We didn't think those commies would make a move like that, but Uncle Sugar's got it covered."

"He'd better," the first said. He peered over at me with appreciation, and then extended his hand. "Bygones?"

"You got it, first," I said. We gripped each other's hands like men. He had a pretty good bonecrusher, but so did I.

"I'm going up to the bridge to help navigate us out of this mess," I said.

"I'll stay down here to organize the crew," the first said. "That is, if AB Pepper will allow that."

"Given your wartime service, I'd say that you'd be ideal for this, Commander," Pepper said. They shook hands, too. Pepper shook the hurt out of his hand afterward.

I climbed back up to the bridge. The captain stood alongside the AB there, his hand on the seaman's back.

"I'd recommend zigzagging," I said.

"I know how to avoid submarines, mister," the Skipper

peevishly replied. And that's when we heard the loud thud and subsequent explosion. The bucket immediately listed 45 degrees to port and I felt myself pitching backward. The last thing I remember before blacking out was the panicked look on the Skipper's face, as the cherry-scented pipe fell from his open mouth and clanked onto the deck.

Adrift!

I awoke to the buzz of an outboard motor, smacked awake by repeated jostling up and down as the flat-bottomed dinghy navigated the waves, piloted by Charlie Oats, a fellow third mate who, in ordinary times, was in charge of the ship's galley. Oats had a crazed look in his eye. "We're getting away!" he shouted above the sound of the motor. He stared up at the sun.

"From—?"

"The end times!"

My head was ringing, and all his shouting and the

slamming of the boat on the waves wasn't helping. "How —?"

"Flying saucers! G-darned flying saucers! That's what's going on!"

The sun pounded down. We'd cook on this rubberized nightmare if we weren't careful. Was this the boat the hapless Soviets had used to travel over to the *Mother's Mercy*? It had to be. Our lifeboats had wooden hulls. We hit a high wave and I flew into the air, flipped over and landed facedown on deck. I grabbed a handhold and pulled myself up, kneed my way over to Charlie. I clapped him on the arm. "Let me drive for a while."

"Sure," he shouted, giving me a jimmy-eyed glare, half-blinded by staring into the sun. "You drive!"

I grabbed the rudder, which also acted as the throttle for the engine and slowed the boat down to a crawl. I looked behind our escape vessel and saw nothing but blue sky and ocean. A similar vista appeared starboard, port and forward.

"You're not going fast enough. Gimme!" He crawled back to where I was. I killed the engine.

"What the hell's going on, Charlie?" I gave him a sharp push on the chest, knocking him backward.

"While you been getting your beauty sleep? Plenty!"

"Do you see anything around us?"

He stood up on his knees, peered around, his pudgy, liver-spotted hand shielding his pointy little eyes. "Could be a submarine."

"That submarine wasn't interested in us. Those Soviets were interested in the cargo."

"You're crazy!" He pointed a stubby finger in my face. "Crazy!"

"Did you talk to them? I did. They wanted something we had in the hold."

"Damned Russkies!"

"Take a load off, Charlie. Relax a moment and tell me how I ended up on this boat."

"How do you think you got aboard? I pulled you in here after the *Mother's Mercy* cracked in half."

"Anyone else survive?"

"How should I know? I got the H-E-double-hockey-sticks outta there as soon as possible." He looked up into the sky, squinted and stared directly into the sun again. "Boy! That sun, huh?"

"Yeah." I clapped him on the shoulder. It was like slapping a rump roast. "You've been through a lot. Take a breather. I think we got far enough away from them at this point."

"Sure, sure."

On the port side of our little vessel, I spied a sheet-metal box, seemingly glued to the fiberglass deck. I popped it open and found a flare gun, a canteen, a first aid kit, and a metal can with a pull-top—all of it adorned with Cyrillic script. I was still groggy. I closed my eyes for a moment and felt the waves lap below us. Charlie was right about the sun. It was a killer.

Quick as a wink, Charlie reached into the toolbox and swiped the canteen. He was plenty fast for a fat man. I turned in time to watch him chug-a-lug the only fresh water for miles. By the time I grabbed it back, he'd nearly emptied the canteen. All that was left for me was a hot swig. Charlie was going to be trouble.

"You owe me your life, you know," he said, as I swirled what was left and then drank it down.

"Thanks, Charlie. You always could fry up a mean omelette, too."

"I do fantastic things with powdered eggs. Amazing."

"We should head south."

"Who put you in charge?"

"I'm the navigator."

"You *were* the navigator. Now you're just as stuck as I

am on this R-A-F-T." He reached over the side and splashed some water on his face. "Stings." He was a blonde-haired, blue-eyed, pink-complected dope, built like a fireplug. I had to figure out how to get some shade for him before he cooked in all this sun. He was dressed similarly to me, in khaki, but with cook-stains splotching his armpit-soaked shirt. Two of his shirt buttons were missing nearest his considerable gut, and his white undershirt showed through, stained haze gray and yellow. "Bleach," I thought. His boondockers, like mine, were scuffed and waterlogged, rimmed with salt from foot sweat and our recent dip in the ocean. Neither one of us had a drop of oil on our bodies. That was a mystery, too. Surely, when the boat cracked open, fuel and oil spewed all over the place... right?

Up ahead was the answer to that question. "Is that what I think it is?" I pointed.

Charlie turned around. "It's a just a bunch of flotsam."

"It's the remains of our ship."

"Naw! It's a garbage patch. There are plenty of them out here. I run across a couple since we made our getaway."

We drifted up to it. "You've been going in circles." I turned around, unscrewed the gas cap and checked out the fuel situation. We had about a drip left.

"Circles? You're full of beans!"

We came closer to the former cargo of our former ship, a lot of it floating due to wooden storage crates. An oil slick shimmered on the surface. I pulled in the first crate we came across, marked MOLASSES. I tore it open, and sure enough, there were a dozen glass flasks of black-strap molasses inside nestled in some very wet straw.

"Nice haul!" Charlie said, sitting there on the bow, his legs crossed at the ankles like he was in his favorite easy chair back home.

I pulled in another crate, this one larger— CALIFORNIA ORANGES, with a beautiful vista painted on the label. I dumped the oranges onto the floor of the raft and kept the crate. I had an idea how I could use it.

I found a gray tarpaulin with six metal grommets, one of which had a length of rope tied onto it. Perfect. I pulled it in. I found a Brooklyn Dodgers ball cap and fished that out, shook the oil off it. I held it in my hands. "Poor first," I said aloud. "Jesus."

Charlie sat up. "Is that the first's hat?"

"You should put it on. It would keep the sun off you."

"I hate the Dodgers," Charlie said, proudly. "I'm a Giants fan." He slapped his chest.

"Fine. I'll wear it." I put it on. It was a slightly loose fit, and still a bit waterlogged.

"I thought you was from Chicago."

"I am."

"Traitor." He picked up one of the oranges and peeled it, tossing the rind over the side. He chewed down the orange in short order and made himself comfortable in the bottom of the raft, a thin layer of fiberglass between us and the deep ocean.

I picked through the oily wreckage like a gal shopping at the A&P. We floated away from the wreckage, some small bits of which were still smoldering. Not a human being around. Not a peep. I stood momentarily in the raft. "Anyone out there? Hello! Mates?" It was depressing that only Charlie and I seemed to have survived. But if that was the case, where were the bodies? You'd expect to see them. Maybe the Soviets snatched up our guys... or maybe our Navy did. That was slightly less depressing to think about. The Navy couldn't be far. Flare gun? No, I'd save that for when I got a visual on them. Unlike many soldiers I knew, I had nothing against the Navy. They'd saved my ass a couple of times in the Philippines. I certainly would have been happy to see a Navy ship at that moment. Overjoyed.

Charlie fell asleep on the hard floor of the raft and snored like a buzzsaw. I slipped one of the bottles of molasses in my pocket for safekeeping. I took the empty canteen out of the toolbox and slipped it behind my back. One bottle of molasses could probably provide me sustenance for a week. And I could fill up the canteen when it rained next. I pulled apart the length of rope, separated it into several smaller strands, and made a mast out of the orange crate, reusing the nails and gluing it together with molasses. Soon enough, using the tarp, I'd rigged up a sail. We could sail at night, I figured, and drift with the tide during the day, using the tarp as cover from the sun. We'd head south, using the Southern Cross and the stars Rigil Kent and Hadar to the left of the Southern Cross to navigate by. The woolen Dodgers hat shrunk to fit on my head as it dried.

I made a fishing rig using some more of the rope twine and a small nail from the orange crate. Tiny fish were gathering under the raft, attracted by the shade.

Water would be the biggest problem.

The sun dipped down below the horizon and the wind picked up. It was pleasant and calm out on the ocean. Charlie awoke and rubbed his eyes. "How long have I been sleeping?"

"You needed it."

"You're gee-darned right, I did." He looked around at all my work. "Nice S-A-I-L."

"Thanks." I pointed out which direction we were heading.

"You got it all figured out," he said suspiciously. "Almost like you'd *planned* for this to happen."

"Of course I have it figured out. I'm a mariner."

"Big boss man in charge. You're only a third mate, like me."

"I'm hoping for some rain," I said, trying to change the subject. "Get some fresh water."

Our wet clothes dried. A salt crust formed on them.

"Sure, sure," Charlie said, smacking his lips. "I'm feeling a bit parched myself."

We sailed along pleasantly, save for the lack of water. The evening was cool. I caught a small fish. Inside the first aid kit, I found a pair of sharp scissors and cut the fish apart in the lid of the box.

"Raw fish," Charlie said, smacking his lips. "Just like Japan."

I peeled one of the oranges and squeezed a segment on top of it. "Ceviche, like in Peru."

"Nice!"

I baited another hook with some of the guts. I caught one fish after another using the same method until we had our fill. I steered by the stars. Maybe this wouldn't be so bad after all, I thought. We needed rain, though. The water contained in the fish and oranges wasn't enough. My eyes stung from the salt spray. I wasn't part of the deck department, but as a mariner, I'd seen the corrosive effects of salt on metal. I could only imagine what it was doing to us.

Fat and happy, Charlie leaned back and studied me, his stubby hands laced behind his head. "You got a G-A-L back home, Russo?"

The wind was picking up a bit and the sea began to chop. The stars were disappearing in the horizon. "By God, I think we're about to get some rain!"

"You a queer or something?"

"What?"

"Don't want to talk about your girl?"

"I'll talk about her later, Charlie. Help me pull down the sail. We're gonna need her to collect some rainwater."

We pulled the sail down quickly, and put my makeshift mast on the floor of the boat. The wind picked up. I tied the tarp to the handholds just in time, as we tossed up and down in the churning ocean, threatening to flip over at times. The rain came in buckets, washing us both down, and the tarp. I emptied out the toolbox and, after the fish guts washed out of it, I funneled the precious water off the storm-cleaned tarp into it, and surreptitiously into the canteen, which I stowed behind my back again. I drank deeply off the tarp and so did Charlie, as we were tossed about recklessly by the roiling ocean. We were specks out here—mere dots compared to the vastness of the Pacific! I felt, strangely, free. Freer than I'd ever felt in my life. The ocean calmed down to a light chop and the sky cleared, revealing a new morning. Exhausted from hanging on for dear life, I fell into a sweaty sleep.

Buy Me a Drink, Sailor?

I dreamt of my girl, my former girl. She was never my girl, to be honest. Not really.

I met Geraldine McGillicuddy in the summer of '49. I saw her out of the corner of my eye while nursing a cold one at the Salty Squid, a sailor dive near the port in Frisco. She was stacked like Jane Russell, her raven hair framing her perfect face, as she sipped a lady drink, amber booze in a high-stemmed glass with an umbrella and a stack of cubed fruit pierced on a tiny plastic sword. She sat perched on a stool at the other end of the bar. We shared a glance that became something more. Maybe a look of recognition, like we knew each other from somewhere or sometime else. I slid into the stool next to her.

"Buy me a drink, sailor?" she said, conversing with herself. "Sure. By all means. Buy me a drink."

What could I do? I bought her a drink.

We talked for a while, and it was like I'd known her all my life. We laughed. What did we talk about? I don't remember exactly. I remember the beat of my heart in my ears, the rushing of blood through every inch of my body. We're made of seawater and I felt like the sea was inside me, calm on the surface and roiling underneath. She excused herself to go to the ladies. I watched her walk away like she was a circus performer on a tightrope, one foot in front of the other, her heels clicking on the wooden floor to the beat of my heart, her legs going up a mile to her too-short skirt, which swaddled that delicious bottom.

"Mother of mercy!" I said to the barkeep.

"Run," he said, wiping a beer mug clean with a bar rag, a toothpick jutting from the side of his cigarette-pinched mouth. "Run as far and fast away from here as you can. That one's trouble, mac. With a capital T!"

I should have listened. But how could 1 listen? I couldn't hear a thing but my own breath catching when she came walking back from the head, her breasts bobbing about in her pink sweater like a pair of puppies fighting in a sack.

She plucked the Chesterfields out of my pocket, tapped out two, and placed them in her lips, painted the color of a ripe plum. I fumbled around in my pocket for my Zippo. She steadied my hand with one of hers as I lit the cigarettes. Her touch was electric, her hand soft, her nails perfectly manicured with the same plum color shellacked on them. She slipped the rest of the smokes back into my pocket. She took a puff and blew the smoke out of the corner of her perfect mouth, now inches from mine. She placed the second lit cigarette in my lips and I tasted her mouth for the first time. She turned my hand so she could look at the crest on the lighter. "Dragoons?" she purred, plucking the cigarette from her mouth with her perfectly manicured free hand.

"Forty-eighth infantry regiment."

"Army or Marines?"

"Army."

"Oh," she said, with a slight bit of disappointment leaking through. "See much action?"

"Enough," I said, and snapped shut the lighter, slipping it back in my pocket.

She talked about her old boyfriend, Cheyenne, a cow puncher from Wyoming who, from her description, was approximately seven feet tall and was as handsome and sculpted as a national monument. She'd met Cheyenne on the docks when he'd come home from the Pacific, his chest weighted down with medals, telling stories of killing most of the Japanese army on Okinawa with his own two bare hands, with some occasional help from a handy entrenching tool and a Colt M1911 that he fired from his hip. The absent Cheyenne was an impossible standard to live up to, so I didn't try. I had no desire to talk about my experiences in the Pacific. When I thought about some of the things that circumstances forced me to do, I felt revulsion more than anything else.

She'd come to the coast from Albuquerque with a dream of becoming a model for *Eyeful* magazine, or maybe *Glamour*. She allowed me to walk her home to her apartment, which she shared with a redhead named Gladys, who, when we arrived together, warned her repeatedly about the landlady's policy on bringing home strange men, especially sailors. Gladys stalked around the apartment in a hairnet, shimmery bathrobe and high-heeled slippers with a powder-puff glued near each toe. "He's a tall one," Gladys finally said, slipping into an easy chair and appraising me as I stood around wondering if I should sit, or make my excuses and go. I finally sat on the couch and lit a cigarette and took a long drag. I looked around and found no ashtray on the pine end table or the pine coffee table, both scored with scratches, like a bored tomcat had found them interesting. An old radio dominated the room, the kind we all used to listen to when Roosevelt was president, trying to calm us all down about the state of our ruined country. Some big band music came out of the thing, tinny.

I waited for Geri to reemerge from her room. She had a portfolio of her modeling that she wanted to show me. Like I knew anything about that. Or about anything. I knew how to steer a ship. I knew how to fire an M-1. I wasn't good for much of anything else.

Gladys crossed her legs and smiled over at me. They weren't bad legs. Not bad at all. "You're kind of handsome. But you know that already, don't you?" She smiled sadistically and sadly. "She'll never love you, sweetheart. She'll never love anyone but Cheyenne. I'm not even sure she loves him. I think she loves the *idea* of him." She scissored her index and middle fingers at me, and I tapped out a smoke, lit it for her and placed it in her hand. She'd stolen some of Geri's plum nail polish, but it had begun to chip. I went into the kitchenette and dug around in the sole cabinet in there, found a tea saucer with a little rose design in it, like something Grandma would own. We shared that as an ashtray. "Go pour us all a drink, will you sweetie?"

"A man's work never ends." I found a bottle of Old Crow, three mismatched tumblers and poured out drinks. "I'd've made a mixed drink, but I don't know how."

Gladys sighed. "I'm parched. Hand it over."

I sat on the part of the couch nearest her. I decided that Gladys was all right. I might even be attracted to her if there wasn't a knockout in the next room. Gladys could sense this. I imagine that this sort of thing happened a lot. "Here's to you," I said, and clinked glasses with her.

"Aw! You went ahead and started the party without me!" Geri said from the doorway, perfect hands on perfect hips. She'd changed into something more comfortable, or at least easier on the eyes. She was dressed similarly to Gladys, minus the hairnet, but the robe hung on her body in a way that left just enough to the imagination that my mind sizzled.

"Va-voom," I whispered aloud.

"I gotta get my own place," Gladys said, disgusted, taking a puff and a swig. "I'm outta the competition around this dump." She stood up and finished her drink, stubbed out her cigarette. "See you in the funny papers, chum." She went to bed.

Soon enough, so did Geri and me.

Things went like that for a while. I'd come back from

sea, and come knock on her door. She'd be waiting for me, gussied up. I'd take her out for a good Porterhouse and some fine whiskey, and she'd talk about modeling or Cheyenne. Mostly Cheyenne.

Cheyenne had knocked up some go-go girl in San Diego. The go-go girl made the journey up the coast to Frisco and convinced him to do the right thing and marry her. "He'd bought me a diamond ring and everything!" Geri said, her voice filled with the rage of the smitten and rejected. In retrospect, I'm sure she wasn't used to being rejected. She was used to wrapping a man around her pinkie finger, the way she had me. But where was the challenge in that?

We lasted about a year until I was called back into active duty after Truman decided to go all-in in Korea. I had orders to report to Fort Benning, where I would train infantrymen. I wouldn't have to go fight. Something about a point system. I don't know.

I asked Geri to marry me, to come with me. "We've had good times," I said.

"I've had good times with a lot of men," Geri said. She rolled over from me so I could look at her perfectly curved back leading down to her overripe bottom, bare and sweaty. "You're not so special."

"Not like Cheyenne," I said.

She rolled back over, her eyes filled with excitement. "He wrote me last week! He said that he didn't get married! That go-go girl got the little mistake taken care of by some croaker in Wyoming after she saw where she was gonna have to live. I grew up on a ranch. I can live on a ranch."

I got up and put on my shorts, pants.

"Aw! What's the matter? Why you gotta leave already? We were having fun."

"See you around," I said, knowing that I wouldn't. I put on the rest of my clothes.

She got angry. "Don't forget your shoes!" and she threw them at me, one then the other.

I caught them. "Thanks." I sat down on a chair near her vanity and put them on.

"Cheyenne is twice the man you are!"

"So you've told me," I said, and I walked out the door.

As it turned out, I barely spent a month at Fort Benning. Old Man Konrath contacted the Department of the Army and told them I was needed back at sea to deliver supplies to the Far East. They agreed and let me go.

That broad got inside me. She camped out inside me. She wouldn't leave, no matter how much whiskey I drank to try and wash her away. I spent years moaning about her to shipmates and shore buddies alike. I'm sure she didn't give me a second thought after I walked out the door.

Shark Attack!

"Ceviche!" Charlie shouted, waking me. "You're a commie queer! I knew it from the git-go!" He'd made a crude tent from the tarp and the makeshift mast and sat Indian style opposite from me, next to the outboard. The flare gun shook in his hand, pointed in my general direction. He'd hog-tied me with some of the rope. There wasn't an orange to be found. His lips were brine-crusty. His teeth were purple. The toolbox was open and dry. The canteen lay at his feet, top unscrewed. The can from the metal box was open, and half of the beet slices from it were still sloshing around in there.

"What the fuck, Charlie?"

"You've been sick and muttering for a day! 'Jerry! Jerry!' What kind of sick F-U-C-K has a crush on Jerry Lewis?"

"That's Geri. G-E-R-I. She was my girl. She left me, you dumb asshole. Or I left her. Not really clear on that, to be honest. Now untie me!"

"You'd like that, wouldn't you? So you could bugger me in the A-S-S with your commie dick! You led that sub right to us, didn't you? And now you're navigating to meet with it and turn me over to your queer commie masters!"

How can you argue with someone as dumb as a box of rocks? "You need me to survive, you idiot. Clearly, you haven't been doing okay on your lonesome."

The Dodgers hat was shoved unneatly onto his oversized noggin. He threw off the hat, disgusted. "How can you wear this hat? It doesn't even fit a normal head!" Keeping the flare gun leveled at me, he reached over and picked up the canteen and held it over the side for a moment, lifted it to his mouth and chugged.

"You gotta be kidding me! You're a mariner. You know that the last thing you're supposed to do is drink seawater!"

"You drained all the gas, you commie J-E-R-K! The engine won't even turn over!" He dropped the canteen on the fiberglass deck and gave the cord a few pulls to demonstrate. "What have you got to say for yourself?"

"I say that if I get out of these ropes, I'll wring your neck, you fat fuck. You've killed us both."

"Oh, ho-ho! You won't be getting out of the knots I tied, you limp-wristed Russkie L-O-V-E-R!" He sat back, pulled the tarp away from his head and looked up at the sky. "Albatross!"

I peered upward and saw nothing.

Charlie stood up, unzipped and pissed over the side of the boat. "It's a nice day to be at sea!" he said, triumphantly. "I'm the captain of this boat. Me! Skipper Oats!"

He'd done a bang-up job on the knots. It took me all of five minutes of fiddling around to untie them. I played possum, closed my eyes... mostly. I watched him. He sat down again, and again dipped the canteen into the sea. He lifted the canteen up to his sea-split lips, and I pounced, slugging him right in the wattles. Unfortunately, he squeezed the flare gun's trigger and blew a hole in the side of the boat. We tipped over, the boat fell quickly apart—there's your Soviet workmanship for you—and Charlie began sloshing about. "I can't swim!" he whined. And he thrashed harder.

I could swim, and I quickly backstroked away from him. I saw a fin, and then another, and slowed down, trying not to attract the attention of the sharks, who now circled Charlie. The fish swimming in the shade underneath the boat must have attracted the sharks to begin with. "Save me, you red queer!" Charlie wailed, as the first shark struck him. Another shark, and then another came after him. Soon, I saw a slick of blood and gore replace what used to be Charlie Oats.

I bumped into something hard, and turned around. It was a massive, wooden crate, labeled in drippy, blood-red stencil, "FISH." I climbed on top of it and lay down, the sharks circling, bumping into the crate.

A blob of white goo splattered on my shirt. I squinted through the sunlight and saw the albatross floating above me. Land couldn't be far away. I sighed in relief, still sick and feverish, not to mention completely dehydrated. I got on my hands and knees and saw the island off in the distance, green and black, with a swirl of white smoke rising from its highest peak into the blue sky above. The Brooklyn Dodgers hat floated up to me, along with one of Charlie's fingers. I flicked the finger off the bill and put it on. The hat fit perfectly.

I collapsed facedown and passed out.

Island Girls!

I awoke, tiny splinters in my jaw, with a thirst that could kill a rhino. I opened my eyes and saw the most beautiful face I have ever, or will ever, see. It was a girl, 20 years old, with a pair of dancing pale blue-green eyes flecked with gold, a pert little nose, and a cascade of jet-black hair that glistened in the sun. Her pink mouth was open like she'd found a puppy under the tree on Christmas day.

"I love you," I said involuntarily. What else are you going to say to a face like that?

"It's a man!" she squealed in delight. "Oh, and he's a big one, too! I pulled him and out breathed the life back into him! I call him first! He's mine!"

"You can't call him!" another girl's voice called out.

"I can, too! Find your own man!"

My eyes came into focus and I propped myself up on my elbows. The FISH box was nowhere in sight. I was on a beach filled with coal-black sand as fine and soft as talcum powder. I peered around. I was surrounded by beauties. There had to be almost a dozen of them, all of them with hourglass figures, curly hair, and not a blouse to be found.

They all wore nothing but grass skirts and rings of bright pink flowers around their wrists and ankles. They were crouched down, hands on beautifully dimpled knees, resembling Ava Gardner, if Ava was as brown as a nut. They had breasts as round as coconuts, and as jiggly as fruit-filled gelatin fresh out of the mold, little blackish-brown nipples poking out.

The original girl was the best of them. I couldn't stop looking at her. Her smile was like some sort of crazy drug. Her eyebrows arched up quizzically. I became fixated on her beaming countenance. God help me, I wanted to kiss her glorious ripe lips and the tiny cleft on her chin! I wanted to hold her in my arms and feel the warmth of her. "Hi," I said.

"Hi, yourself, handsome! You ain't French, are ya? Papa Wally says we aren't allowed to talk to Frenchmen."

"I'm an American," I said. "Chicago born."

"Oh, Chicago! Papa Wally is going to be so pleased t'meetcha! He used to carry a lot of water in that town. And then we'll get married! Do you want to marry me?"

"Yes!" I said quickly. I'd never been so certain of anything in my life. I had a vision of living in a suburb with her, our little brown children dancing in the sprinkler while she sat in my lap sipping a glass of ice cold lemonade.

"You have to get me a ring! That's part of getting married! That's what Papa Wally says."

I reached into my pocket and found the bottle of blackstrap molasses, miraculously unshattered. I handed it to her. She quickly unscrewed the top and stuck a delicate brown finger in and then sucked the molasses off it in a way that caused me to audibly groan. She screwed the top back on and put it in a gunny sack she was carrying like a purse. "This 'Papa Wally' sounds like a smart character."

The girls all giggled.

I tried to stand up, and then found that I couldn't, and stumbled back down into the scorching hot black sand. I lifted my burnt hands from it quickly and dusted them off on each other, sitting up. "I think I need a moment."

"Take your time," my betrothed said. "I didn't catch your name."

"Russ. My friends call me 'Russ.' It's Russell Russo. How can you stand in your bare feet in this hot sand?"

"Mrs. Russ Russo!" she shouted, a giddy giggle bursting through the words. She hopped up and down clapping her hands, her beautiful breasts bobbing. "Eat your hearts out, girls!"

"We're supposed to share!" one of her sisters called out. A lot of the rest of the girls crossed their arms, hiding their bountiful bosoms. One girl had red hair cut into a bob. Another was blonde.

"Where did you all come from?" I asked. "How come you speak English?" They sounded like they were from the Midwest.

"Papa Wally can answer that," my girl said. "Papa Wally can answer any questions you like."

"He's real smart!" one of the other girls said. She was tiny, almost precious looking.

"Yah!" two of the girls shouted in unison. "Real smart!" They were copper like a pair of pennies.

Another girl, the blonde, produced a glass bottle filled with fresh water and handed it to me. I chugged it all down with abandon. "There's plenty," she said. "Don't choke. Can I have a kiss now?"

"Get your own man, Sandy!" my girl said, pushing her away. She crouched down, leaned over me and ran her delicate fingers through my hair. "My name's Heena." She smiled again, beatifically. She was an angel. Her grass skirt rustled as a cool tropical breeze blew past us. Waves crashed on the shore. She might as well have been the only girl on the beach.

"Heena," I whispered back to her, like it was a secret. I felt an unfamiliar tremble go through me.

"Heena Russo," she said, trying my name on for size.

"I must be dreaming. This is some sort of dream," I

said. "Delirium."

"Uh, oh!" one of her sisters called out. "The boys from the other side of the island are over here. Pick up your spears, girls, and let's get'm!"

Heena leaned over and kissed me gently on the lips. It was electric. "Be right back, hun! Don't go nowhere." She picked up a spear and made a high, keening noise in her throat that went, "Yi-yi-yi-yi-yi!" and charged, bamboo spear aloft, toward the jungle. I managed to get to my feet in time to see a motley collection of awkward Polynesian men, also in grass skirts, go sprinting off in the opposite direction. One of them was wearing the blue Dodgers hat.

Through the Jungle!

When she and the other girls came back, I noticed they had managed to cover themselves a bit more, mostly with floral arrangements. They each wore a crown of red flowers and a necklace of pink ones. Heena glowed among them, like the brightest star in a constellation. It wasn't her build—they were all pretty much (gloriously) built the same—as much as the way she carried herself. And that face! They kept their bamboo spears in woven holsters attached to their grass skirts. They all had gunny sack purses.

"Paradise," I said, my chest filling with helium. "This is what they mean by 'paradise.'" I scratched at the beard that had developed on my face. How long had I been at sea? I still couldn't be sure if this was real or not. If it was a dream, I didn't want to wake up.

Heena beamed up at me. She was maybe five-nine, with long, muscular legs. "You're even better standing up," she said enthusiastically. She ran her hands across my torso. "Mmm-mmm-mmm! You're all muscle, don'tcha know!"

"Sure. Russell Muscle."

"No fair, Heena!" one of the girls said, this one taller than the rest.

"Dottie, you're not getting him," Heena replied. "He loves me, and I love him and we're going to make babies and lots of them! And they'll all be tall! Real tall!"

"You always get your way! I'll tell Papa Wally on you!" Dottie said, peevishly.

"Tell it to the seagulls, buster!" Heena said. "Won't change a thing. Isn't that right, Russo?"

I scratched my big dumb head and said it again—again involuntarily: "I love you."

"See, Dottie-Dot-Dot-Dumbo!" Heena took my hand in hers, and turned toward the other girls. "Go make love with one of the jungle soldiers! Or the boys from the other side of the island. Or those Frenchmen with the talking monkeys!"

"Talking what? Did you say talking—?"

"Don't worry your pretty head about it, loverboy. I'll take care of you," Heena said. She blew me a kiss with her free hand and squeezed my hand hard. "I'll take extra good care of you."

We walked into the jungle. I blindly followed them down a well-worn path, still holding Heena's hand. I should have been starving, but her mere presence seemed sustenance enough. The girls sang a song while we tromped down the path:

Oh, we ain't got a barrel of money,

Maybe we're ragged and funny!

But we'll travel along, singin' a song,

Side by side!

A while later, I felt fatigued and slowed down in a wide clearing.

"Are you hungry, hun? You look famished! Build my man a fire and cook him some fish!" She clapped her hands twice and the other girls scattered into the jungle in a flash.

I pulled Heena close and kissed her waiting mouth. She wrapped her arms around my neck and pulled herself up to her tiptoes. I put my hands on her grass-covered hips and rustled the grass skirt away. I caressed her bare bottom with the tips of my fingers. I was alive in a way I hadn't been in so very long. I tickled her tongue with the tip of mine and she pulled back and slapped her hands on rhythmically on my chest like she was beating on a pair of bongos, looking both appalled and excited. "Oh my gosh! Do girls like that thing with the tongue back in Chicago?"

"They do, darling. They do!"

"I think I'm going to like it, too. Do it again!" and she leapt up and wrapped her arms around my neck and her legs around my waist. She chipped a sliver off my incisor with one of hers. We french-kissed for a long minute. I felt dizzy afterward. She slipped back down to the ground, fanned her hands in front of her face and rolled her eyes. She turned and sprinted up a coconut tree like a squirrel, retrieved a coconut, and sprinted right back down, while her sisters arrived with firewood. They produced fish out of gunny sacks. Heena bashed the coconut neatly over a sharp outcropping of rock, tossed the husk over her shoulder, and handed me the coconut. She sat down by my feet and looked up at me.

"I need a minute," I said, plopping down next to her. I drained the coconut water and set the coconut down.

She took my hand in both of hers and covered it with kisses. She placed my hand over her heart, between those bountiful breasts, her fingers caressing the back of my hand and her thumbs tickling my wrist. "Take all the time you need, big fella."

It was like ten thousand volts were going through my mitt. "Mother of mercy!"

A flying fox swooped past, with a body as big as a cocker spaniel and the wingspan of a MiG. It slammed into a nearby fruit tree and then, a moment later, hung there upside down. Everywhere I looked, there was fruit falling from the trees! I realized I was starving, yet I couldn't get up. It would mean leaving her side, and I couldn't do that, I knew, and still be able to live.

"Heena, where are we? What is this place?"

"You're on Mondo Tiki Island in the middle of the Pacific Ocean. We've got a volcano and everything."

"Mondo Tiki?"

"Oh, the island god. He's a fickle fella. Sometimes he throws hot boulders at us when he gets good and mad."

She let go of my hand and I reached up and caressed that beautiful face. She kissed my thumb as I stroked her lips. The girls started the fire and gutted the fish. "I'm having a hard time believing this is all real."

"Oh," she went, getting to her knees and stroking my face in turn. "I can't believe you're really real. That's the honest to Mondo truth. I prayed to Mondo Tiki to send me a man... a real man! Not a Frenchman, or a jungle soldier, or one of those icky fellas from the other side of the island." Her eyes lit up and I swear the gold in them twinkled like the stars over the Pacific at night. I was breathless. I forgot how to breathe.

"You okay, sweetie?" she asked solicitously.

I snapped out of my reverie. "What's a jungle soldier?"

"Oh... them! They live in a cave not far from our village. They're all sad and homesick. Their leader is a tall, angry man in black with one glass eye." She circled her eye with her index finger and thumb to demonstrate. "Oh, and he's got a skull on his hat! Papa Wally gives them rum to chase away the boys from the other side of the island. I'll tell you this on the QT: They're not very respectful of women. But they're afraid of us, too. We're bigger than'm, and they ran outta bullets a long time ago."

"Rum?"

"Papa Wally is a bootlegger, don'tcha know. The best bootlegger in America! Used to work for some fella named Capone who shot folks with a tommy gun." She demonstrated the tommy gun by turning both her hands into pistols, one behind the other, winking an eye, and blowing air through her pursed lips, raking the imaginary machine gun side to side. "Papa Wally can make booze outta anything. 'Good thing we have sugar cane here,' Papa Wally always says."

"So Papa Wally is an American. Like me."

"Yah! That's right. Do you know of Fond Du Lac in the land of cheese?"

"I've heard of it."

She rested her head on my shoulder and gripped my bicep with both of her delicate, yet powerful hands. "Thank you, Mondo Tiki!" she shouted toward the steaming mountain that towered above the jungle, above everything. "Thank you for this gift of beefcake!" The volcano rumbled slightly in reply. She took a deep breath, sighed and then waved her hand in front of her face. "Whew-ee! When we get to the spring, I'm going to give you a bath. Do you like having your back scrubbed?"

"Yes," I said, perking up. "Yes, I do."

Campfire Girls!

After a dinner of yellowtail snapper, garnished with papaya and passion fruit, we lounged around the fire as the jungle and the girls chattered away. The other girls winked and flirted with me, but I only had eyes for Heena.

Heena was the youngest of the girls, I found out. She was the last girl born to Papa Wally's fourth wife. The other daughters crowded around me were Dottie, Ruby, Sandy, Irene, Betty, Franny, Lizzie, Judy, Gloria and Louise. Louise was the shortest one at barely over five-foot. She had a sweet smile. Franny and Lizzie, the ones with copper hair and copper skin like a pair of coins, looked the most alike, and didn't leave each other's side. Ruby and Sandy were almost as tall as Dottie. The three of them were around six-foot. Judy sat studying everyone else. She was almost as tiny as Louise, and was the loner, or maybe she was just shy, and barely spoke. Gloria drew pictures in the sand. They were all between the ages of 20 and 29, I guessed.

Papa Wally apparently liked to sow his seed. Four wives and he wasn't even from Utah! Couldn't wait to meet the guy. I figured he must be built like a stallion.

The girls were as chipper as they were beautiful, save for unchipper Judy. They were terrific company. They sat around the fire like they were at a hootenanny. Betty pulled out a ukulele and strummed. They all sang along:

No one to talk with,

All by myself,

No one to walk with,

But I'm happy on the shelf

Ain't misbehavin',

I'm savin' my love for you

It felt so cozy. I didn't realize how desperately lonely I'd been. I'd spent a good deal of my life in the company of men aboard ships, and before that in the Army. Men are raised to be taciturn and direct in the U.S. We're no damn fun. I couldn't remember the last time I was the only man around so many women. I felt myself blushing uncontrollably staring at these gorgeous, half-naked pin-up girls come to life, their bodies slick with coconut oil, wreathed in flowers as big as funnels, wiggling their bare toes in the warmth of the fire.

Betty climbed to her feet, as did Franny and Lizzie. The girls quieted down. "Ready?" Betty asked her two sisters, Franny and Lizzie, to stand up because it was story time. Franny and Lizzie seemed like they'd been shined to a warm glow with a chamois.

"Ready!" the girls said in unison.

"Once upon a time," Betty started, fingerpicking her ukelele.

"Whoosh!" all the girls sang. Franny and Lizzie swung their hips, rattling their skirts, and made waves out of their hands and arms.

"Mondo Tiki, and his brothers Buster and Billy, chartered a fishing boat from Al, the god of the rackets."

Lizzie and Franny pantomimed a transaction, still swaying their hips.

"Buster and Billy thought they were only going fishing, but Mondo had other plans. He was going to cast his net into the deep blue ocean and pull up a treasure that he'd left down there, away from the Feds and their prying eyes. The box was filled with booze and diamonds and winning numbers from the numbers racket. So while Buster and Billy fished, Mondo secretly pulled up his haul!"

Lizzie made a great show of pulling, while, with her back to Lizzie, Franny pretended to whistle and fish with a rod and reel.

"But the treasure got buried, so Mondo pulled and pulled! Soon, he'd pulled up a whole island!"

Lizzie slapped her hands on her cheeks in surprise, and then Franny turned around and looked surprised in turn.

"The island was so startled to be born, it threw up a little and spat hot rocks at the fishing boat. 'We'll never get our security deposit back!' Buster and Billy shouted in dismay."

Franny shook her fist at Lizzie, while Lizzie made a great show of looking just as shocked as Franny, shrugging her shoulders with her palms out.

"Buster and Billy shouted, 'When Al, the god of the rackets, finds out, he'll have us rubbed out! You've gotten us into trouble for the last time, Mondo!' So while Billy waved a gat at him, Buster threw Mondo into the mouth of the island."

Lizzie turned around, and Franny pretended to pick her up by her non-existent shirt collar and by the seat of her non-existent pants and throw her. Lizzie fell to the ground, rolled on her head, momentarily exposing her flawless bottom, and made it back to her feet in a deep crouch.

"Now in complete control of the mouth of the island, Mondo became angry at his brothers!"

Still crouching, Lizzie flattened the palms of her hands together as if she was about to pray, and in one motion leapt into the air and swept her hands high above her. She landed on her feet and swung her arms above her like she was swimming into the sky.

"Mondo said, 'Security deposit, hell! I'll sink that boat with you two bums in it. You better get a wiggle on!"

Franny pretended to drive off, while Lizzie continued air swimming and leaping, her breasts bobbing and copper hair flying about crazily. Betty accompanied all this by playing a fast tempo version of "Sourwood Mountain," as Franny drove her imaginary boat in circles around the two of them, leaping over the fire as she went. They stopped suddenly and all three girls stood facing us.

"And that's how the island was formed and the volcano became gigantic. And Mondo Tiki lives in the mountain to this day, with his booze and diamonds and winning numbers. Sometimes he gets drunk and throws a rock and sometimes he gets plain old angry, so angry that the top of his head steams he's so angry! The end!"

The three girls bobbed a curtsy, accepted our applause,

and sat back down. The volcano rumbled its appreciation.

Jungle Soldier!

"We'll stay here for the night before heading back to our village," Heena said.

"I have no problem with that."

"It can get a bit cold out here at night. We all like to snuggle up together."

"I have no problem with that either."

The girls all crowded around me. I rolled over on my side and faced Heena. Irene spooned up behind me, placed her cheek between my shoulder blades and put her tiny hand on my hip. I gathered Heena into my arms. The light from the campfire threw sparks in the sky around us. As my eyes closed, the last thing I saw was Heena beaming at me, our nose tips touching.

The jungle chatter and the jungle scent awoke

something inside me, memories that I'd bolted down and tried, unsuccessfully as it turns out, to discard. I sat up abruptly in the dark of night, saw that the fire had gone out, and bumbled out into the jungle from our little clearing in search of firewood. My night vision has always been excellent, and the full moon was high in the sky, casting a pale light through the canopy of trees above, so I had no problem navigating around.

I had a full bladder, so I unzipped and pissed on a tall, spindly tree, leaning up against the trunk with one hand to steady myself. I still felt a bit shaky. I heard rustling not far off and spotted someone moving. I thought it was a nightmare come to life, but the vision was real enough. It was a Japanese soldier not ten feet away standing on a log, wearing the Brooklyn Dodgers hat. He had a poorly trimmed beard. His body half-filled his uniform, his too-baggy trousers were held up with a belt made from woven palm fronds. His boots and leggings were scuffed and torn. He held in his hands a long, wooden, bolt-action Arisaka rifle with a rusty bayonet affixed. His mouth was agape in surprise and his eyes filled with terror. "G.I. Joe!" he gasped out, and backed off the log in a half-leap, half-stumble, turned and sprinted away, galloping through the dense brush.

I realized I was pissing on my boots and re-aimed, finished and shook. I zipped up and forgot why I had come into the jungle in the first place. I felt just as stunned as that ragged soldier had looked. "Jungle soldier," I muttered to myself. "Fuck me in the heart."

I stumbled back to our encampment to the sight of those eleven beauties slumbering peacefully, save for Irene, who was sitting up, her arms clasped tightly around her knees. She looked sadly aggrieved. I sat down on a rock and she got up and sat down next to me. She was such a tiny thing. She couldn't have been half my size. "You're sad," she said.

"Actually, I don't think I've ever been happier."

She patted my forearm. "That's the saddest thing I've ever heard. What's a 'nip'? What's a 'flare'? What do you mean by 'pour it on' and 'they're breaking through'?" Her eyes were moist, her forehead crinkled.

"What makes you ask that?"

"It's what you were saying in your sleep. I should've brought my teddy." Did she mean for herself, or for me? She got up and stepped between the bodies of her sisters, found a spot and snuggled in amongst them.

I went back out into the jungle, found more wood, and brought it back. I slipped my Zippo out and lit the fire. I found a spot a few yards away from them. I patted myself down and found no smokes. Turned out I didn't miss them that much.

Soft Nudes for a Repressed Sailor!

The sun cascaded through the treetops and poured down through the clearing. The girls were all prancing around, grass skirts rustling, singing and gathering fruit. They were lithesome and jiggly, like curvy ballerinas. Heena seemed to be the coconut specialist. She traipsed up and down the trees as easily as I could walk on the deck of a ship.

They were used to me now, mostly. I wasn't used to them. Their near-nudity was shocking to someone brought up in the States and in the Catholic Church. We're a country founded by Puritans. I thought at that moment that if the Navy came to rescue me, by some odd chance, and I had the opportunity to take Heena back to the States, she'd have a lot to get used to.

Hell, we probably wouldn't be able to live back in the Midwest. We sure wouldn't be able to live in the South. She was dark enough that people would assume we were a mixed-race couple, which would get our house burned down. In fact, we were a mixed-race couple. Just like her parents.

Maybe we'd raise the kids to worship Mondo Tiki. Tiki seemed like an all right kind of god, given that he'd fixed up Heena and me. My Catholic God didn't throw hot rocks, but He was always threatening me with hell for minor infractions. I would certainly go to Catholic hell for the thoughts I was having about Heena.

We sat around the embers of the campfire crosslegged, eating fruit and drinking water out of old green-glass bottles that had been stoppered with cork. We slurped coconut water, too. I found that I didn't miss my morning coffee. There are all sorts of things that civilization makes you think you can't live without, and then you find, when those things are taken away, that you didn't need them to begin with.

"We should get going," Dottie said, standing up. She was the oldest and the tallest at maybe six-foot-one. She was very protective of her siblings, gathering them together and making sure they holstered their spears, slung their gunny sacks, and that Betty didn't forget her ukulele, which hung across her back on a long, brown-leather strap that seemed like something off a Sam Browne belt. Maybe it was.

Heena took my hand and we walked side-by-side, traversing the jungle path behind her sisters.

"Did the American Army ever come through here?" I asked her.

"Ask Dottie," Heena said. "She remembers all that stuff."

I gave Heena a kiss and said, "I'll be right back."

"I know," she said, and smiled that narcotic smile, the one that made me gasp for breath and my heart rattle like it wanted to escape from my ribcage.

I wended my way to the front of the line, excusing myself as I slipped past each girl and receiving more than one pinch on the buttocks as I scooted along. I made it up front and asked Dottie my question, and she gave me a long look out of the corner of her eye. "We waited for them," she said, her voice taking on a dark tone. "But they never came. *You* never came. Why didn't you come?"

"It was called 'island hopping.' We skipped islands that couldn't accommodate an airbase, or that didn't have strategic value."

"'Strategic value'? What's that?"

"It's not important. The war's been over for ten years."

"Not important!" she said, and snorted out her disgust. "Breeze off, beefcake! Heena can have you. Stay here and wait for her." She gave me a little push and I nearly fell off the path.

I stopped, and the girls all slipped past me, pinching and poking at me, except for Judy, who shielded her face with a tiny brown hand that didn't look like it had a bone in it. Betty, her ukulele strapped on her back and a smirk on her lovely face, even made a grab for my groin. I jumped backward and landed in the bushes, as the girls laughed musically. Louise, who looked like a doll come to life, made a pouty face at me. And then Heena came up, bringing up the rear. She took my hand again and we walked leaning into each other. I slipped my arm across her shoulders and her arm looped around my waist. We were like a pair of lovers taking a promenade on the lakefront back home. We were so caught up in each other that we lost the girls a couple of times and had to jog to catch up, but not before stealing a few kisses.

Into the Spring!

We stopped at a massive spring filled with crystal clear water. A waterfall poured down from an igneous rock formation. Tropical birds chattered in the trees surrounding us. The girls lifted up a rock and pulled out homemade bars of soap that smelled like coconut meringue pie. They also pulled out woven mats that they laid out on the many boulders surrounding the spring. They slipped off their grass skirts, flowers, gunny sacks and spears and dove into the water completely nude, soap bars in hand, and washed each other down. Dottie remained standing on a rock, spear in hand, standing guard.

"Jungle soldiers," Heena said when she saw me looking at Dottie. "They hide out in the jungle and watch us, don'tcha know. Sometimes they steal our skirts. Ruby says they take them back to their caves and sniff'm." I turned and looked at Heena. She was nude, and her beauty was jawdropping. "Time for your bath, Russo." She smiled at me mischievously, and then looked down at my very present erection. "Is that for me? Oh, boy!"

She and I peeled off my filthy boots, khakis, socks. I left on my boxers until I waded out waist deep into the water, and then peeled them off. I tossed the sodden trunks to the shore. We went under the waterfall and into the area behind it. She kissed me deeply and passionately. I caressed the breasts that I'd been staring at for so long, and her nipples popped out to greet my fingertips. I reached into the cleft between her gorgeous thighs and gently stroked her with the tips of my fingers, watching her face as it went from surprise to pleasure to ecstasy as I discovered her pleasure spots. Her head went back and she cried out, "Russo!" I ached for her. She expertly guided me inside her, and we made loud, passionate love. "Mondo Tiki-Tiki, Mondo-ohhh!" she cried out, as we came in concert. It was everything I'd imagined, and more. The volcano rumbled off in the distance, as if applauding our efforts. We panted, exhausted and I sat down on a rock with her still straddling me. What she was doing with my cock while I remained inside her was nothing short of extraordinary.

"You're not a virgin." It didn't feel like an accusation when I said it, but it came out that way.

"I've fooled around." She frowned when she saw my expression. "Nothing serious! Only with one of the Frenchmen when they came ashore. And there was a real sad jungle soldier for a while. But none of them kissed me like you do! They didn't look at me the way you do, either! I always make sure that it's after I've had my monthly visitor." She patted my chest. "Sex is a basic human need, Russo, like water, fish and fruit."

I shook it off. She was right. My American mores had no place in this steamy tropical world. "Sorry for that. It's the way I was raised."

"It'll only be you and me from now on, Russo," she said, giving me a wet smooch and slipping off me, her body shimmering like a seal. "And if I catch you with one of my sisters, it'll be lights out. Got that?" She shook a warning fist at me.

"Got it."

She picked up the bar of soap she'd brought with her. "Turn around. It's time for your scrubbing." She did it all manually, and then allowed me to do the same with her. That body! She was a relief map of heaven! We dunked into the spring and came back up, clean. She was hairless from the neck down. I'd never seen a woman like that before. The answer how came fairly quickly. She picked up a sharp shell about the size of my hand and soaped and shaved herself, and dunked again. "Your turn." She soaped up and shaved my face, and then started on my genitals.

"Whoa, whoa!" I went.

"Hold still. I don't want to cut you." She very carefully shaved me. It felt... odd. Then she took me in her mouth, and I understood! God, how I understood! She (and I) finished, she spat and said, "Your turn." I picked her up, placed her on the rock and went to town, her legs over my shoulders. She opened up like a flower—a Georgia O'Keefe thought, I guess. When in Rome! "Russo, me-oh, my-oh!"

After taking the measure of each other's passion, and washing again, we emerged from the waterfall exhausted, and yet energized. "Paradise!" I said aloud.

Ruby, so named (I take it) because of her bobbed red hair, stood watch on the rock, while Dottie bathed. The rest of the girls were sun-drying on the woven mats, all of them naked as they day they were born, glistening with coconut oil.

We waded over to my clothes. I pulled out my wallet and lighter before washing my trousers. I didn't even need a cigarette after sex on this magical island. I washed my clothes with the brick of soap, swishing them in the water, and laid them out on one of the boulders. I noticed that all of the girls were similarly clean-shaven, all eleven of them, baking in the sun.

The rest of the world could go to hell as far as I was concerned. They'd have to drag me out of this place, kicking and screaming.

Ruby shouted, "Jungle soldier!"

Sure enough, it was the little guy I'd seen the night before. He scampered out, snatched one of the grass skirts, and nearly made it into the jungle when the still nude Ruby tackled him from behind like Chuck Bednarik taking down Frank Gifford. The little man shrieked in both pain and, possibly, rapturous happiness. Without looking, she tossed the grass skirt backward and Sandy (the blonde one) caught it. Then Ruby snatched the Dodgers hat off his head and tossed that back to Sandy.

"This yours?" Sandy called over to me, waving the hat.

"Yes!" I said, not untruthfully. It had become mine. I

slipped on my still-damp BVD's and walked over to retrieve it.

Ruby had the Japanese soldier on the ground when I got there, a knee in his back. She leaned down and said in his ear, "Are you sorry?"

"So sorry!" he said. She smacked him on the keister. "Oh, ho-ho!" he went with obvious pleasure.

"Better not let me catch you snooping around here again, Hiro!"

"You won't. I promise." He was hyperventilating with fear and glee.

She let him up and he turned around and gave her an appraising look. She grabbed him by the shoulders and kissed him on the lips, and then shoved him away. "Beat it, buster. Scram!"

Yeah, he'd beat it all right. All night back at the cave. "See you, Ruby-baby," he said, and sprinted off into the woods.

"Where's his rifle?" I asked.

"He never brings it with him. Leaves it leaning on a tree," Ruby said. She dusted herself off, slapping her hands across her delicious, jiggling body. "Jeez, will you look at me? I gotta take another bath."

"I'll scrub you down," Sandy said. She handed me the ball cap, and I put it on.

I watched them wade out into the water, while Dottie retook her place on sentry. "This sure beats anything they have on the DuMont Network," I said to myself.

I walked back over to Heena. She handed me a half coconut shell filled with clear, viscous fluid. "Oil me up, willya?"

"With pleasure."

French Chimp!

The girls put on their grass skirts, picked up their gear, and after they were duly inspected by big sister Dottie, we headed off on the trail again.

My clothes were soft and comfortably clean thanks to the scrubbing they'd gotten. I felt human. More than human, considering the company I was keeping.

"Almost home!" Heena said. She gave my hand a squeeze.

We strolled along the widening trail, and emerged from the jungle into a field of sugar cane. The stalks were over six feet high, green at the top and brown at the bottom, all well-tended and in very neat rows. I could see over the top of it, barely, and saw blue skies overhead and steam billowing out of the peak of Mondo Tiki, the active volcano that loomed over us.

From behind us, I heard a rustling in the cane field and turned around. Heena unholstered her spear and dropped into a crouch. "Stand behind me," she snapped when I started walking toward the rustling stalks. She grabbed my forearm with her free hand and jerked me backward. She was shockingly strong.

I stopped and stared into the greenery, and pushing his way out was a tall chimpanzee, strolling on his legs, as erect as a human being. He was chewing on a bit of sugar cane, smacking his lips and showing his teeth and pink gums. He wore a beret on his noggin. Underneath, barely concealed, I could see shiny metal, maybe stainless steel. The chimpanzee looked over at us and coughed into his fist. "Excusez-Moi! Je suis désolé!" the chimp seemed to say. He hid the sugar cane behind his back and surreptitiously dropped it, giving it a little kick backwards.

"Did that chimp just speak? Did he just say something?" I looked around at all the girls, and they all were not surprised in the least by the speaking chimp. They seemed annoyed.

"Get behind me! They seem real nice, but they only want to eat our sugar cane and try to make time with us!" Heena said.

"He's not so bad," Irene said. "He wants love, like anyone else."

"Mon nom est à César! Ma chérie, ne pas avoir peur," the chimp seemed to say. He couldn't be talking, could he? He removed the beret and I could see a helmet on his head, and wires that appeared to be sparking. He held the beret in both his hands in a supplicating manner. He took a step or two toward us.

"Back off, ape!" Dottie shouted from behind us. She sprinted up with her spear at port arms, and then she brandished it at him, giving him a bit of a poke.

He backed up. "Mon amour, tu me ramener chagrin," he seemed to say. My mind kept rejecting this… this ape! This chimp! Apparently speaking French! He sounded like Louis Jourdain, or maybe Pepe Le Pew.

I'd learned French in college, and tried some out on him. "Allez-Vous en, monsieur le singe!"

"Je suis ton serviteur, monsieur," the chimp said. He turned and bowed deeply to Dottie. "Jusqu'à ce que nous rencontrons à nouveau, ma douce." He replaced the beret on his head, adjusted it to a rakish angle, and bounded like a stallion on his feet and knuckles down the trail, in the opposite direction from us.

"What the hell kind of island are you people running around here anyway?" I asked Dottie.

"Ah, go soak your head," she said in reply, and stalked back up to retake the lead.

Papa Wally's Village of the Gals!

We followed Dottie toward the village. Heena and I were right on her tail. The girls seemed well-suited to handle the chimp if he came sniffing around again.

Dottie was muttering darkly to herself.

"What's that, hun?" Heena asked.

Dottie whipped around and said, "I'm not marrying a monkey! I don't care how desperate I get, I'm not marrying a gosh-darned monkey!"

"Nobody asked you to," Heena said defensively. "Jeez, Louise!"

"What?" Louise went. We didn't even notice her, the little squirt. She'd sidled up next to us when we were unaware. I looked down at her. I wanted to pinch her cute, little button nose. I wanted to hand her a cookie fresh out of the oven on a Fiestaware plate, tell her it was too hot to eat, and watch her wait for it to cool.

"Nothing!" Heena said. "I'm just saying, nobody's asking Dottie to marry a monkey."

The gossip went backward and soon the girls were making little ook-ook sounds, along with, "Have a banana, mon cher!" and "Oui-oui, let's swing from a tree!"

"Put a sock in it or I'll marry all of you off to the monkeys!" Dottie shouted back at her sisters, her fist raised, and they all giggled.

The sunshine, the fresh air, the scent of flowers and coconut oil wafting off the girls, the rustling of their skirts, and their musical voices all made me feel higher that a skyrocket on the Fourth of July.

We came around the corner, and there stood Papa Wally.

Papa Wally wasn't exactly what I was expecting. He looked like a guy I'd bought a lemon off one time on Western Avenue back in Chicago. I drove the car off the lot and it immediately threw a rod. "What did I tell you gals about bringing a Frenchman in here?" he hollered. He was wearing a grass skirt, too, just like the rest of them. His nose and shoulders were as pink as a Virginia ham, his blonde hair flowed off the sides of his head, which was topped by a Panama hat that had seemingly been chewed upon, but not recently, by an enraged chihuahua. His eyes were Wedgwood blue with little streaks of red in the whites, which were gray. Tiny purple capillaries criss-crossed his face like a relief map, and looked ready to burst out of his cheeks and nose. He wore a pair of loafers that had once been white with brass chains, but had been worn down by time and use, and had little patches of fuzzy mold around the toes and the brass chains were as green as Lady Liberty. He had a white-blonde Fu Manchu mustache, the long tips of which threatened to tickle his beer barrel belly, which was covered in white fur as fine as cobwebs. He wasn't an inch over five-five either. He was like someone's sad idea of a debouched South Pacific lawn gnome.

"I'm not French. I'm American."

"Sacre bleu!" He laughed heartily at his own joke. "Where'd you find this one, gals?"

"He's mine, Papa Wally! I called him fair and square!" Heena said. She grabbed my bicep like she was daring him, or the rest of the girls, to try to take me from her.

"She can have him," Dottie said. "He's a drip."

Lizzie and Franny, who I finally realized were twins, shouted out in unison, "Dottie's gonna marry a monkey!"

"Lizzie and Franny are gonna get a sock in the jaw!" Dottie replied.

"Girls, girls!" Papa Wally said, patting his considerable belly. "Did you find what I sent you out there for?"

"Still didn't find that Frenchmen's ship," Dottie said, taking charge. "We'll search further to the west next time. Once we found Mister Man, here," she thumbed over at me contemptuously, "we decided to head on back."

"Russ Russo. From Chicago." I reached over and Papa Wally gave me a good, Midwestern double-pumper of a handshake, exactly like the one the Western Avenue car salesman had bestowed upon me.

"Waldo Bostick. Esquire. I'm the major-domo around here." He licked his lips with a swollen white tongue like he was late for a nip out of the bottle. "Chicago? I used to carry a lot of water in that town."

"Bostick? That rings a bell."

"Heh-heh," Papa Wally went, slapping me on the arm like we were old pals. "Yes, yes, we can talk about that later. Heh-heh!" He leaned in, grabbed my arm and pulled me down toward him. "Confidentially, did you come here on a ship? Is the ship nearby? Does the ship have steak? I'm dying, literally dying, don'tcha know, for a steak. And scotch. I'd settle for the scotch. Scotch!" He enunciated the hell out of "scotch."

"My ship was cut in half by a Soviet torpedo. I may be the only survivor."

"Oh. That's too bad! Too, too bad. Shame. Gosh darned shame. Yes."

Heena took one of my arms, and Papa Wally the other.

We walked into the village, which included a dozen huts surrounding a leering totem that was mostly head, the head being mostly mouth. I looked at Papa Wally, then the statue. There was more than a passing resemblance. "So that's Mondo Tiki?"

"I raised my girls to be good Tiki-ists. Or Tiki-ans. Never really made up my mind about that. They worship the island god. He's all-knowing and all-seeing. Not a lot of speaking, mind you, except for the occasional burst of lava. He's cranky. Needs rum."

"Ah."

"I drink it for him. It's the sacrifice I make."

Heena and I looked at the gigantic wooden idol together. "So that's your god, eh?"

"That's him."

"Pleasant looking fellow."

"Don't patronize my god."

There were four grave markers by Mondo Tiki. His four wives, I presumed. I didn't ask, and no explanation was offered at that moment.

"I was blessed with all girls, except for Wally Junior here."

"Ya-hey," a little squirt said, sitting on the porch of the largest of the huts, the one that said "Papa Wally" on the outside. He was a spindly little fellow, twig forearms resting on knock-knees. Barefoot, grass skirt, chewing on a piece of straw. He was a shade lighter than the lightest of the girls, maybe only a medium tan. He was as blonde as his dad and his sister Sandy. Wally Junior made a gun out of his hand and the thumb-hammer dropped. He winked and clucked his tongue. That acorn didn't fall very far from the tree.

The series of wooden huts circling the idol were constructed on eight-foot-tall hard wooden stilts with high thatched roofs topping the huts like grassy pointed dunce hats. The walls of each hut were composed of bamboo that was wired together tightly and some sort of shiny shellack was applied to make them watertight. Each of the huts had a girl's name painted on the side in a dancing pink script five feet high. We stopped at the one labeled "Heena."

"We're ho-o-me!" she sang out. She turned around gleefully, her breasts bouncing, her pert little nipples saluting.

How can I describe how deliriously happy I was to hear her say that? I can't. The closest I can get to it is the exact moment when, in a field hospital in the Philippines, I knew that I was going to survive and, as a bonus, I was wounded enough to go back Stateside. But that was a different kind of happiness. It was happiness with a gloom chaser. There was no gloom at Heena's hut.

I looked down at her bare feet, dirtied by the trail, and had a sudden compulsion to wash them. It was not a fetishistic urge, but rather bloomed inside of me as a desperate need to perform a romantic act that I could accomplish right away and that maybe no one had ever offered to do for her. Love is strange. I snatched her up in my arms, which made her squeal with delight, and carried her up the steps.

She waved to Irene, "We're gonna make bay-bees!"

"Hurray!" Irene shouted over joyfully.

"Go grab me a pail of water and a bar of soap, willya Irene?"

"Sure!"

I marched to the door of the hut, my girl in my arms, and gave the door a little kick. It was a lot nicer inside than I thought it would be. The interior had a finished basement quality, with white-painted mastic on the walls, and pink accents. She had a little hurricane lamp on a bamboo nightstand next to her bamboo-framed bed, the mattress stuffed with palm fronds, by the look of it. The sheets were silk, made out of parachute material. There was a table in the middle of the room made from a giant spool, with a homemade earthenware pitcher and basin on it. An olive drab field table with a warped mirror affixed to the wall made up a vanity, with an oversized white comb made of a fishbone atop it. There was a window above her bed with no glass, just a shutter that opened up from the bottom with a stick to prop it open.

She even had a few paintings on the wall, mostly of Mondo Tiki, who looked even more like Papa Wally as depicted there. The paintings were signed, in graceful script, by Gloria, who had also painted all their names on the huts by the look of it. The place was a lot nicer than the top floor of the two-flat that my pop rented out, and that he'd once offered me rent-free if I'd come home to Chicago and work in the butcher shop with him. I grew up in the bottom floor, just me and pop. Ma ran off with a jazz singer shortly before the crash in '29. Still have no clue what became of her. She might as well have been abducted by the UFO's everyone was so giddy about back Stateside.

I gently placed Heena on the bed, her feet out.

Tiny Irene lugged in the pail and handed me the bar of soap, and quickly skidaddled, nearly dancing out the doorway.

I washed Heena's feet with my hands. She dunked them in the bucket. I took off my shirt and dried her feet with it.

"How did you know?"

"Know what?"

"Our marriage ritual."

"Oh? Are we married now?"

"You still gotta get me a ring. But, yah!"

"Give us a kiss, Mrs. Russo."

We kissed.

Not on the Ship!

We loudly and exuberantly consummated our marriage and afterward, in each other's nude embrace, whispered to each other of our love.

"I'm afraid I'm going to wake up and find that I'm back on my ship."

"You're not on your ship. You're here. With me."

"I didn't think I was capable of this. Not anymore."

"You seemed pretty capable a few minutes ago, Russo."

Happy Po-Po!

I'd put on my clothes and wandered outside to take in the

air while Heena slept through the afternoon in our little love nest. The sun was inching down over the horizon, and the sky turned purple and orange through the ash billowing out of the island god's mouth. I ran into the major-domo himself.

"Al once said to me, 'There are no small men, only small ideas.' Or maybe it was the other way around." Papa Wally mumbled each to himself for a moment. "Anyway, whichever one sounded more profound, that's the way Al said it."

"He died of syphilis."

"Well, Al always did love the dames. Me, too, as it turned out."

"Yes, you sowed your seed very successfully."

"It wasn't always like that," Papa Wally said. "When I first came here, the island was lousy with natives. Lazy bastards, too. I kept asking them to dive for pearls for me. That's why I came out here. The pearl trade. But you know what these native birds had to say to that?"

"Beats me."

"Taboo! Taboo! Their religion wouldn't allow them to go pearl diving? Taboo, my sweet behind, says I. As luck would have it, I had a case of the Spanish flu. I survived, but most of the natives didn't. Some sniffly boys survived, if you can call the lives they live survival. Would have married any number of them off to my girls, but those lunkheads started up with that taboo junk, too. Frankly, I don't think any of them can swim. So I exiled them. Bring me some pearls back, I tells'm, and you can come a-courting. I find them bumbling around out in the jungle sometimes and have to chase them off with a stick."

"Life of Riley," I said.

"What's that?"

"Nothing."

"Say, you're a big fella, aintcha?"

"Sure," I conceded.

"How would you like to participate in a public works project? An important one."

"Always glad to pitch in."

"Good to hear you say that, sonny boy!" The wily old coot disappeared into a nearby utility shed, also made of bamboo and thatch, and emerged bearing a shovel. He pointed out the current outhouses, one marked "Ladies," and the other marked, "Gents." "Seems the ladies' is overflowing. Imagine that."

"Uh, huh. Want me to dig a new one, do you?"

"If you wouldn't mind."

I would mind, but didn't say so. I took the shovel from him. I'd dug more than one latrine during my Army years, so was familiar with the work, such as it was. I took the shovel and made my way over to the outhouses, stepped off about 20 paces, and dug through the thick, green moss and into the rich, basaltic soil. A few hours later, I was about four feet down, the hole itself being almost four feet across. My military mind caused it to be perfectly square, as if a large cube of dirt had been lifted out of it. I was sweaty and filthy. I looked up and saw my bride standing there with a basin of water.

She crouched down and placed the basin next to the hole. I stood the shovel up by its blade and walked over.

"Look at your trousers! Do you see why we wear grass skirts? They don't hang onto the dirt they way your clothes do. Take off your clothes and I'll scrub'm down for ya."

"What? Right here?"

"Did you get shy all of a sudden, Russo?" She smiled knowingly at me.

"I'd rather go back to the hut." I washed my hands and face in the bowl. My hands stung from popped blisters.

"My po-po is very happy," she said, tilting her head just so. She caressed my forehead with the tips of her fingers.

"Your po-po?"

She lifted her grass skirt and reintroduced me to her delightful po-po.

"So… let's go back to the hut," I said.

Half Savage, All Woman!

We went back to the hut. By the time the sun went down, we'd consummated the hell out of our marriage for a second time. While I lay on my back on the bed, sweating and aching from both of my days' labors, Heena washed my clothes and hung them up to dry. "Papa Wally used to wear clothes like this. Sometimes, he pulls them out and puts them on. I think he will tonight. We're gonna have a wedding feast!"

"More fish and papaya?"

"No, no! Dottie speared a wild boar this morning while we were making bay-bees! It's been roasting in a pit, don'tcha know. She put the molasses you brought on it."

"So that's what I've been smelling all day." I propped myself up on my elbows.

"Be right back!" Heena put on her grass skirt and nipped out. She returned with the bucket and a bar of soap, made me stand, and washed me down. She picked up a shell from her vanity, and shaved me again, and was very careful, especially down south of the equator.

She took the bucket away again, and came back. It was my turn to wash her and she allowed me to shave her. At the end, we lay down together for a few minutes, until Irene knocked on the door and entered. Irene took a long, lingering, unashamed, appraising look at me, and then handed two armfuls of leis made of frangipani to Heena. Too late, I covered my genitals with my hands. Heena dumped the leis on the spool coffee table, turned around and said, "You've had your look." Irene was still staring. She licked her little lips. Heena turned red-faced and shooed her away with her hands. "Beat it!"

Irene smiled demurely at me, cocked an eyebrow, turned and left.

"She wants to have babies, too," Heena said. "But

she'll have to find her own man. Maybe a jungle soldier. Or maybe another fella will wash up on the shore."

"I think we'll see more Americans here soon."

"That's what Papa Wally said when we were kids, after the old ones died, but it didn't turn out to be true."

"The old ones?"

"Yah! The savages. I'm half-savage, y'know."

"Couldn't tell." She sat down next to me on the bed and rubbed my belly with her soft hands. "What happened to the old ones?"

"Oh, they got real sick and died. Most of 'em before I was born. The boys on the other side of the island used to live here at first, but when they got old enough to want to make babies, Papa Wally chased 'em away."

"So Papa Wally was the first white man here, I take it."

"Nah. The boys on the other side of the island? They learned English from a couple of missionaries. Y'ever heard of Erie, in the land of Penn?"

"I have. So these missionaries. What happened to them?"

"Papa Wally gave'm their walking papers. What's a walking paper, anyhow? Never understood that."

"It's just an expression. It means he told them to leave."

"Oh? Yah, they left all right. But they left behind all their books. Mostly bibles and a complete set of the *Encyclopedia Britannica*. Y'ever read the bible? It's real confusing. In the first half, this God fella smites the heck out of folks and in the second half, he's a milquetoast who lets a bunch of fellas kill him. Couldn't really relate to the whole thing."

"I'm Catholic, so I have a passing familiarity with the bible."

"Oh? Yah? So what's a Catholic believe in?"

"Guilt and shame, mostly."

"That doesn't sound like a good religion."

"Try telling that to a few million Italians."

"Huh?"

"Give us a kiss, my sweet."

We kissed. I brushed her hair away from her face and we looked into each other's eyes for what seemed like an hour, or maybe only a moment. I forgot to breathe again, and gasped to catch my breath. "You love me," she said. "Yah, y'do! I can tell."

Wedding Feast of the Mondo Tribe!

I put on my khakis and boots, and cocked my Dodgers hat on my head. Heena placed a wreath of flowers about my neck, and then clothed herself entirely in the rest of the flowers—ankles and wrists, neck and waist. "You have to carry me outside," she said. I picked her up in my arms, and we kissed. Then I pulled the door open with the hand under her knees and carefully guided her through the doorway. Torches lit a path to the luau.

The girls followed us down the path, appearing one by one from behind the torches. They sang, as Betty strummed the ukulele.

You are my sunshine

My only sunshine.

You make me happy

When skies are gray!

At the end of the long line of torches, I found three chairs on a bamboo stage in front of a roaring campfire. In the center chair, the highest, sat the major-domo himself, good old Papa Wally, who wore the top-half of a white tuxedo with a high-collared shirt and a black bow tie, a cummerbund straining around his considerable waist. Below that was a grass skirt. He wore shiny, black oxfords with long white socks kept aloft on his skinny shins with sock garters. He wore a yacht captain's hat on his noggin, and had slicked his long mustache with some sort of grease.

I placed Heena in the chair on Papa Wally's left, and sat down on Papa Wally's right.

"How are you two lovebirds getting along, sweet pea?" he asked.

"Swimmingly," Heena replied.

"That's terrific. Wally Junior! Where are you, lad?"

Wally Junior appeared, similarly attired to his pop. He carried two cigars on a silver platter, along with three coconut halves filled with liquor. Papa Wally handed me one of the cigars after biting off the tip, and took one for himself and likewise bit off its tip. I pulled my Zippo out and lit his first, and then lit my own. Ah, tobacco! Every cell in my body cried out in relief.

"Don't get used to it, sonny. It was a present from the Frenchies."

I took a couple of puffs, let the tobacco roll through my very being, and then carefully put the cigar out and shoved it in my shirt pocket.

Heena took one of the half-shells and Papa Wally and I took the other two. "A toast!" Papa Wally shouted out. "A toast to my new son-in-law! May the two of you be forever happy, and make lots of babies together." He leaned over to me and muttered, "Boys this time, I hope." The girls settled in around the fire. Papa Wally clapped twice quickly, and Betty, Franny and Lizzie stood up. Betty strummed a little on her ukulele. It almost sounded like "Foggy Mountain Breakdown." Franny and Lizzie did a little high-stepping dance while she strummed, swinging their hips, high-kicking their legs and humming along. It was an incredible display of virtuosity.

"Did you teach her that?" I asked him after she finished, to a round of applause from everyone around the fire, and even a few people hiding out in the jungle nearby, who I'd assumed were the ever-present jungle soldiers or boys from the other village. Possibly both.

"I taught her a few chords, but she really made it up all

on her own. She makes her own strings from god-knows-what."

I took a swig from my coconut shell and the stuff inside was pure jet fuel. "That'll clear your sinuses," I said.

"And how!" Heena said, and took a swig from hers. "Whew!"

Papa Wally had already finished his and was jiggling the container at Wally Junior, who uncorked a fresh green-glass bottle and poured his pop a stiff one. "Want another?" he asked me.

"Why the hell not?" I said. And Wally Junior topped me off.

Heena wisely waved her impish brother away.

Chicago Overcoat!

"And now our national anthem," Papa Wally shouted. We all stood up, and Papa Wally smirked and winked at me. The girls all turned toward the flames, hands on their hearts, and sang sweetly and sincerely…

Roll out the barrel, we'll have a barrel of fun

Roll out the barrel, we've got the blues on the run

Zing boom tararrel, ring out a song of good cheer

Now's the time to roll out the barrel, for the gang's all here!

We ate great heaps of pork, sweetened by molasses, off of veiny green leaves as big as platters. We also had fried plantains and cubes of multicolored fruit, and I drank more of Papa Wally's potent rum than I should have.

Sated with booze and food, we sat back in our seats and watched Betty, Franny and Lizzie put on another show.

"Whoosh!" the girls all went.

"Listen, listen, listen and I'll tell you a story! It's a story about Mondo Tiki before there was an island, in the beginning times. Mondo Tiki was born in the upstairs flat above a speakeasy," Betty said, strumming along with herself. "He snuck out of his mama's womb and went to make time with the girls downstairs and try his luck at the craps table. When he came back upstairs, he was a boy already, and his mama didn't recognize him in his pinstriped suit and snap-brim fedora. 'Mama, it's me! Your sonny boy!' Mondo shouted."

Franny pushed Lizzie away.

"But his mama wasn't buying it. Soon his brothers Buster and Billy chased him out of the house, shouting, 'Scram, you dewdropper! You better hightail it outta here!'"

Lizzie ran around the fire, leaping as she went.

"He had many adventures around town, but running the numbers for Big Al was the best of them, and he made plenty of cabbage, and brought it home in a sack. His ma became more understanding after that and let him stay in the flat."

Franny hugged Lizzie and pantomimed taking a sack from her. She licked her thumb and counted a stack of money, flipping through it with glee.

"So the four of them settled in above the speakeasy, but Mondo noticed that his ma was slipping out every night. Mondo wondered where she was going, but he couldn't keep his eyes open. So he tacked up some thick drapes to the windows so his ma would oversleep, but he didn't. He stole her clothes, too, so she couldn't get too far. His ma *did* oversleep, but she used some magic and made everyone believe she was wearing clothes and slipped out of the house."

Franny dropped her grass skirt and, nude, crept away from the fire. A few catcalls came whistling in from the jungle. Lizzie followed her stealthily, pretending to hide behind trees.

"Mondo followed her across town to a social club, where the boys were all playing pinocle, and couldn't see her nudity because of the magic. But before he could see who she was meeting, Mondo was chased away by some of the goons. 'Kids don't belong here!' they shouted, and cussed him out real good."

Lizzie backed away with her hands up and went back to the front of the fire. Franny ran back over and put her skirt back on.

"When he got back home, Mondo said to his brothers, 'Ma keeps sneaking out at night. Ain't you the tiniest bit curious about where she's going?' And Buster and Billy said, 'That ain't none of our business, pal. Why don't you mind your own?'"

Franny gave Lizzie a shove.

"Every night his mother snuck out, and every night Mondo followed his naked ma to the social club. Finally, one night, he turned himself into a pigeon and fluttered in. He saw that his ma was with Big Al himself, canoodling, but he had to scram before the goons turned him into squab."

Nude again, Franny hugged herself, making smooching noises, while Lizzie flapped her arms and danced away.

"He went back night after night. Finally, he couldn't stand it no more, so, high in the rafters above his ma and Big Al, he took a big pigeon crap on Al's forehead. Al picked up a bottle of Canadian Club and threw it into the rafters, striking Mondo and Mondo fell to the ground. The feathers disappeared and Mondo was a boy again. Al said, 'Ain't you that kid what runs numbers for me?' 'What of it?' Mondo asked. 'Why you taking a crap on my head, kiddo? I oughta put you in a Chicago overcoat!' And Mondo's ma shouted, 'He's our son, that's why! Don't you touch a hair on his head!' And Al instantly forgave Mondo and quickly gave him a cut of the numbers racket. His mother hugged him and said, 'That's my boy!' The end!"

While she played both Al and ma, Franny leapt back and forth dropping and picking up her skirt. At the end, she was nude again, and bowed with her sisters. One of the Japanese soldiers shouted from the jungle, "Hotsy totsy!" and came dashing out, only to be subdued by two of his comrades, who tackled him and dragged him back into the bushes.

I attempted to give them a standing ovation, but found I was too drunk to stand up, and only half stood before losing my footing and flopping backwards into my chair. In the distance, the volcano rumbled and bright red sparks shot out of the top like Chinese fireworks.

Papa Wally leaned over and slurred out to me, "I had four wives, and all four of them passed away in labor. Heena's ma died giving birth to that little slip." He gestured toward Wally Junior, who was sitting at his feet.

"So they're all buried next to the totem?" I asked. I was three-quarters of the way into the bag myself.

"Nah," Papa Wally said. "We took them up to the volcano, had a nice little ceremony, and tossed them in. The girls all believe that their mothers are living with Mondo Tiki now, waiting for a reunion in the afterlife. Religion is full of useful little lies, ain't it?"

Kidnapped!

Dottie shook me awake. I was hungover like nobody's business, my head pounding like an anxious banker on an Okie dustbowl farmer's door. "Wha—?" I slurred out.

"Where's your wife?" Dottie asked.

"Ugh," I went, feeling around on the bed and finding

no one there. I sat up and shook the cobwebs away.

"Drink this, beefcake," she said, handing me an earthenware mug. "Then follow me." She turned on her heel and stomped out the door.

I drank the disgusting mixture and then, moments later, projectile vomited out the open window. I spat and wiped my mouth with the back of my hand, and instantly felt much better.

I stumbled to the door and squinted through the sunlight, watching Dottie striding purposefully toward the site of the previous night's luau. I was fully clothed and had no recollection of how I ended up in bed. It wasn't like me to drink until I blacked out. I'd done it a few times at the hospital back in California, but hadn't since that time because, I told myself over and over, I was better.

I jogged down the path after Dottie, and came up alongside her. Sandy and Ruby were already there, hands on hips, looking more than a little angry. Ruby tossed me an empty canister about the size of a beer can. "What's it say?" she asked me, her bobbed auburn hair fluttering a bit in the fresh breeze drifting across the island.

I read, "Gaz de Sommeil" on the side of the can. A warning label read, "Attention, provoque la somnolence dans les 10 mètres!"

"Out with it, Mrs. Grundy," Sandy said. "It's those

Frenchies, ain't it?"

"It's the French all right," I said. "This is a can of knockout gas."

"While you were all spifflicated last night, those Frenchies made off with your gal and our sisters!" Dottie said. "I say, let's go get'm!"

Sandy and Ruby each punched their own hands.

"Let's give'm a dose of medicine!" Ruby said.

Sandy growled like a panther.

"How many girls did they grab?" I asked.

"It was Judy and Heena. They were cleaning up last night," Sandy said. "I shoulda stayed out here with them."

"If big boy here wasn't on a toot, he woulda stayed out here," Ruby said.

"Yeah, I get it," I said. "Let's stop shooting the breeze and get a move-on. I got some Frenchmen to punch in the chops."

"Attaboy, beefcake!" Dottie said. "Follow me."

Lair of the Frenchmen!

We tromped through the jungle, double-timing it to the lair of the Frenchmen. What we found there was astounding. There were no girls, just three men sitting around a small circular table on folding chairs, smoking out of a shared pack of Gitanes. They all wore white linen suits with skinny black ties. One of them, the fat one, had a pith helmet resting on his knee. The others wore straw pork pie hats, cocked on the backs of their heads. They were all mopping their brows with handkerchiefs.

Behind them was a beige canvas tent the size of a small house. Paper lanterns were strung on wires from the trees.

When I charged out of the jungle, they stood up. The fat one said, "L'Américain! It is, how you say, a pleasure to meet you at—" And I slugged him in the chin, causing him to tumble backward.

"How… vulgaire!" said one of the others. The two of them stood up and backed away.

"Where're the girls?" I said. "Out with it!"

The tubbo pulled a metal gizmo with a dial on the front of it out of his pocket, extended a shiny antenna from it and gave the dial a twist. In a flash, I heard the shrieks of a dozen primates ringing out. Soon they surrounded us in the trees and on the ground. They sauntered up.

"Call off your apes!" I said. "And give us back our girls!"

"We don't have your femmes, monsieur," said the taller of the two pork pies.

"Then what's this?" I tossed him the empty can of knockout gas.

"Ah! I can see your confusion, mon ami. We have hired these... how you say? Aborigènes? To do some tasks for us. They asked, in return, for a few things that we have around. I assumed the sleeping gas would be used in hunting, not for kidnapping these... femmes magnifiques."

Dottie, Sandy and Ruby walked out of the jungle and gave the apes in their way a poke or two with their spears from the non-business side.

Tubbo picked himself off the ground. The other two doffed their hats and bowed. The three of them put their headgear back on. Tubbo said, "We are being rude. You must excuse us! I'm Doctor Maurice Thuilière, and these are my traveling companions Yves Manglou," the taller one bowed, "and Jean Marcel," and the shorter one bowed. "Cigarette?" Tubbo said, handing me the pack. I took one and lit it with my Zippo.

"So who has our sisters?" Dottie asked, and then she screamed a little and leap up when one of the apes pinched her bottom.

She slapped him, and the ape said, "Excusez-moi, mon cher." He backed away. It was the one from the field, the ape who called himself César.

"How much longer we gotta barber around with these monkey-lovin' jerks, beefcake?" Dottie asked. "Gimme five minutes with that one over there and I'll have him singing 'Yankee Doodle Dandy.'"

All of the apes had the metal skull caps sparking on their heads. "Where's my wife? Where's her sister? I'm asking politely now. See how polite I am? My politeness could win an award. Don't upset the femme magnifique over there. You wouldn't like her when she's angry."

"We appreciate that. Truly, we do," Jean said. "Your name is?"

"I'm Russ Russo."

"And what brings you to our little island, Russ Russo?" the Doc asked. He placed his pith helmet back on his head.

"A commie torpedo and an ocean breeze. Where's my wife?"

"All in good time. Ladies? Please come join us! We have a tart little Blanquette de Limoux that I think you shall find refreshing. Pierre!" he called out to one of the apes. "Bring us a few more chairs. Richard! Uncork the Blanquette de Limoux! Let it breathe!"

Soon, the apes did as they were told and we were seated around the little round table with the Frenchmen, sipping their alcoholic grape juice and eating tiny crackers gooped over with salty fish eggs.

"We grow tired of our own company, alas. We have been shipwrecked here for too long. It is hard to maintain civilization in such a climate," the doc said.

"Oui," Yves agreed. "And yet we must continue! Persevere!"

"To perseverance!" Jean said, and the three clinked glasses.

Dottie sniffed the wine skeptically, and then drank it down in one quick gulp. Her sisters did likewise.

"These crackers ain't half bad," Sandy said.

I smoked another of their cigarettes.

Sandy said, "Okay. I gotta know. Whose bright idea

was it to wire up those monkey's brains so they could make with the chitchat?"

"Guilty!" the doc said, raising his hand. "One must expand the frontiers of science. Isn't that right, Russ Russo? Americans love to push boundaries in the scientific fields."

"La bombe!" Yves said, raising his glass.

"La bombe!" the doc and Jean agreed, and they clinked glasses again.

"The unfortunate side effect is that our apes figured out how to... escape?" Yves said.

"Yes, and they took over the ship!" Jean said.

"Unfortunately, they had no idea how to drive the ship," the doc said. "I perhaps should have... mistakes were made. Obviously."

"They forced the crew into the lifeboats."

"It was all very sad."

"But they spared us!"

"Oui, even though we tried to get into the lifeboats."

"They said that they wanted to take care of us!"

"Avez-vous pris les filles?" I asked one of the waiter monkeys.

"Non!" said the monkey, as he refilled my glass. "Ce sont les hommes sauvages."

I turned to the girls and said, "The savages have them."

"Huh," Dottie went, shaking her head a bit. "Didn't think they had it in them."

"You speak French!" Yves said.

"Ah, a civilized man!" Jean said.

"Thanks for the wine and the snack," I said, standing up and brushing the cracker crumbs from my trousers. "We have to go fetch my wife and her sister."

"I understand!" Yves said. "Bonne chance, monsieur… et les dames!"

The three Frenchmen stood up and bowed.

"Sorry for the sock in the jaw, doc."

"We are French. We understand passion!" the doc replied.

The Lost Tribe... Discovered!

We crept along the trail toward the encampment of the lost tribe of Mondo Tiki, silently, to the arhythmic beat of jungle drums. The jungle cooled considerably with the setting of the sun, and we could hear, above the din, the sound of waves lapping against the beach accompanied by the chittering and cawing of tropical birds, the rustling of leaves and grass skirts.

"Hoo-hah-hoo-hoo-hah!" came the chant, as light from the bonfire glowed through the branches.

Dottie made the infantry hand signal to stop, and Sandy, Ruby and I each took a knee.

We pushed the foliage aside to witness the spectacle. When my eyes adjusted, I made out Heena and Judy each stripped nude and tied to poles near the fire, off to my right. Neither looked particularly impressed by the proceedings. A six-foot-high by three-foot-wide metal canister loomed to my left. One of the group had attempted to paint a Tiki face on it. It was asymmetrical enough that it appeared that the fire had melted half the face like a wax dummy fried with a blowtorch.

The two-dozen men, such as they were, danced in a sort-of conga line around the two tied-up girls, the fire and the cylinder. I noticed them bumping into each other at regular intervals.

"Sorry!"

"Ouch!"

"C'mon!"

"I can't see through this mask!"

The drumming wasn't even marginally competent. There were three chinless, acne-scarred jaspers flailing on three sets of beaten-to-death drums. They all wore chewed-up, dried-up grass skirts that looked like they'd been run over with a poorly sharpened lawnmower by a suburbanite who'd had one too many Sunday afternoon Tom Collinses. The masks were old and blackened, and would have been frightening on men who stood upright, or had anything like musculature. These guys were fat and frail with stick arms and potbellies. A couple of the ones with the bigger masks on tumbled into each other and fell onto the black sand in front of the girls.

"Oh for Mondo's sake!" Heena went. And the volcano rumbled a bit.

Judy yawned. She pulled one of her hands loose from the ropes, scratched her little button nose, and then slipped her hand back into the ropes.

"Halt!" said the taller of the two mask wearers. The

fellows bumbled into each other like an accordion, or a Mack Sennett comedy. A lot of groaning ensued, along with climbing to their feet and some poor simulations of swearing. The drumming dripped to a stop.

"Okay, okay!" the guy who seemed to be in charge said, his hands upraised. "I'm wearing the sacred mask of Maui Tiki, therefore I get to have sex first!"

The rest of them conferred with each other. Finally, one of them raised his hand. "Not to be rude, but who put you in charge?"

"Pardon me," Maui Tiki said. "I didn't mean to overstep!"

"Not at all," the dissenter said. "I apologize for putting you on the spot."

"We'd all like to have sex! When is the sex happening?" the middle drummer asked in an atonal nasal whine. "Not that I want to be first. I mean, of course I'd like to have a go, but…"

"We'd all like to have a go!"

"Pathetic," Dottie whispered.

"Ever since that big guy got here…"

"Say it, brother!"

"Our odds of having sex have really dropped."

"Disappeared more like!"

"Yeah! He's gonna have all the sex! He's already had sex with Heena a bunch of times!"

"It's only a matter of time before he has sex with them all and sets an impossible standard for us."

"We should kill him!"

"We already discussed that, guys! I mean, that would mean… stabbing him? Or something like that? And then there'd be all that blood and stuff."

"Eww!"

"Remember when we tracked down that boar? And no one wanted to kill it?"

"He looked kinda mean."

"Yeah, and really… who wanted to hurt him? That boar was minding his own business, and we've been okay eating fruit and roots, so what was the big deal?"

"I wish we could fish, but the old ones died before they could teach us."

"Eww! Fish guts!"

"Marty brings up a good point about fish guts."

"When's the sex happening?" the middle drummer whined again. "Not that I want to go first. I'm just saying."

"We're all just saying."

"I'd prefer Judy," Marty said.

"That's because she hasn't had sex with that big guy yet like Heena."

"We all used to have crushes on you Heena!"

"Yeah!"

"I'm hungry," Heena said.

"Can I touch your boobie?" Marty asked.

She rolled her eyes. "Go ahead."

Marty reached out, his hand trembling, and touched the tip of Heena's nipple with his index finger. He immediately retracted his hand.

"What was it like?"

"Magical!"

I stepped out of the bushes, walked over to Marty, and popped him right in his glass jaw, knocking him to the ground.

"We didn't mean it!" Maui Tiki shouted, taking off the mask and backing away. They all backed away from me.

"That really hurt!" Marty said, rubbing his jaw.

"I barely touched you," I said.

This elicited a hail of groans, and more backing away. Dottie, Sandy and Ruby all emerged from the jungle, spears at port arms.

"We didn't mean it!" Maui Tiki said.

"On your knees, you pathetic little worms!" Dottie roared, and they all dropped to their knees. "Beg for your worthless lives!"

"We're sorry, Dottie!"

"Never happen again!"

"We just wanted sex! Is that so wrong?"

"It's not fair that you like the big guy!"

"Yeah! He's mean! We're not mean like him! Why would you want to be with a mean guy?"

"It's not fair!"

"He's a Johnny-Come-Lately! We've put in the time!"

"We gather fruit for you!"

"Why don't you like us? We're nice!"

"Do nice people go around kidnapping their

neighbors?" Sandy asked.

"We didn't have a choice! Ever since your papa came to this island, we've been pushed aside. Us! The real island people."

"He killed our folks with the flu! He owes us!"

"Yeah! Owes us!"

"Let me get this straight," Dottie said. "Because Papa Wally was sick when he got here, and most of the old ones died, that means that we have to have sex with you losers? Do I have that right?"

They mumbled and conferred with each other. "Okay," Maui Tiki said. "That kinda does make us sound like jerks. We're sorry. What can we do to make it up to you?"

"We can gather twice as much fruit!"

"We can gather more firewood!"

"We can tend the sugar cane better!"

Heena and Judy had shucked off their ropes while the fellows debated how to best improve their bootlicking. Judy stood amongst her much taller sisters, crossed her arms and screwed up her face. Heena wrapped her arms around my chest and I held her with my left arm, caressing her face with my right hand. She peered up at me with that blessed face. The gold flecks in her blue green eyes sparkled in the firelight. I kissed her gently on her pillowy lips.

"Aw, no! She's back with the big guy again!"

"Heena will never love us now!"

"We'll redouble our efforts!"

"We'll start working out! Remember that Charles Atlas book that washed ashore last year? We can do that!"

"Yeah! Dynamic tension! Then they'll love us!"

"Hold on, fellas," I said. "Now, aren't you guys supposed to be savages?"

They conferred with each other. Maui Tiki said, "Yes! We are indeed savages!"

"Then isn't it about time you started acting like savages?"

They discussed this point for a while. Leaning forward, his eyes squinting, Maui Tiki said, "Explain."

"Oh for crying out loud," Dottie said. "Let's get out of here. I'm tired. I need something to eat. My feet hurt."

"I'll rub your back, Dottie!"

"I'll rub your feet!"

"We have plenty of food! Have all of ours! We'll gather more. Take a load off. Sit with us for a while. Talk to us."

"Yeah, Dottie! Talk to us!"

Dottie groaned, and exhaled out her exasperation. "Okay. Bring us some food. But none of you goofballs get to touch us without permission."

"Hurray!"

"So you've had men here all along," I said to Dottie, as we watched the native lads scramble around doing their best to please her.

"You call these men?" Dottie replied with a snort. "I could make a better man out of a banana. In fact, I have." I saw her blush when I gave her a look. "Don't judge me, beefcake." We caught each other's eye for a second and both laughed. "Look at them. Mondo on a crutch!"

Marty came over with a batch of fruit and plopped it down in front of us. "Not so fast, pencil neck," I said. He stopped, his back to us. "Turn around."

"What?" he said, once he'd come about. He stared down at the sand. "I asked before I touched her boobie! Don't punch me again!"

"Apologize to my lady."

"I'm sorry, Heena!" He couldn't look either of us in the eye.

"So where did you get the big cylinder?" I asked,

pointing over at it.

"It's our totem," Marty said. "Painted it myself. You think Gloria would like it?"

"No," Dottie said cruelly. "No, she wouldn't."

He cringed a bit, and then peeked up at her tits. "I wish there was some way to make any of you like me."

"No one's making whoopie with you, little man. But I'll tell you what," she said, sitting down on the sand and extending her feet out in front of her. "My dogs are barking. Give'm a good rub and I won't knock your teeth down your throat."

Marty shook with joy. "Oh my!" he went. "I had a dream like this once."

"Shut your yap and get to rubbing."

He sat Indian style by her feet, kissed a small jade idol hanging around his neck on a leather strap, and then reached over with trembling hands and began to rub Dottie's feet. He mumbled something.

"What's that?" Dottie asked.

"I said, 'This is the greatest day of my life.'" He meant it, too.

"Tell me where you found the idol," I said, looking

down at him. But he was too preoccupied to say anything. In fact, I'd say his brain was too fried with joy to form words any longer.

For her part, Dottie enjoyed the foot rub. She peeled a banana that was left in a large pile of fruit in front of her. When she took the first bite, I'm pretty sure Marty ejaculated under his shabby grass skirt.

My nude wife clung onto me. I wrapped my arms around her, and kissed her on the head. "They ever do anything like this before?"

"Never!" she said. "I was a little scared when I woke up and they were carrying me and Judy tied to those poles. They were very angry at you. 'Ruined our chances!' they said. 'Desperate times call for desperate measures!' Then they drew straws to see who got to take off our skirts."

"Where are your skirts?"

"They burned them! Can you imagine?"

I took off my shirt and helped her put it on. I buttoned it up for her, mostly. It was almost dress-like on her, with the shirttail barely covering her bottom, and her tits jiggling around under the cotton fabric.

"Oh, I like you in just your white shirt," she said. She rubbed my chest.

"You look damn good," I said, and we kissed, to a

chorus of groans and boos.

"Yeah, we get it!" Maui Tiki shouted over, his arms filled with various island fruits. "Go ahead and rub it in, big guy!"

"Get over here," I said, curling an index finger at him.

He quickly came over, dumped his fruit at the feet of Sandy and Ruby, who'd also seduced a couple of the lads into rubbing their feet. "Yes, sir!"

"Where'd that cylinder come from?"

"It washed ashore a couple of days ago in a big wooden crate that said 'FISH.' We thought it was fish."

"You're sure of that?"

"Sure I'm sure. We tried to turn the crate into a house. But, um, you know."

"None of you know how to build anything."

"So… right."

"Uh, huh."

I took Heena's hand and we walked over to the makeshift totem, followed by Maui Tiki, his eyes fixed on Heena's wiggling, semi-exposed bottom. On the backside of the cylinder, I found a circular metal badge. In bold print: ATOMIC ENERGY COMMISSION - UNITED STATES OF

AMERICA. In the middle was an atom. "You nosebleeds need to get this thing away from the fire," I said, in my best first mate voice. "Pronto."

The Plan!

I stared impatiently while Marty, Art and Les made bumbling efforts to move the atomic dingus away from the fire. Heena walked over and sat next to Judy and the two of them ate out of the large pile of fruit that the lads were creating.

Art was the name of the character who wore the Maui Tiki mask. Les was the drummer who didn't want to have sex before the others. And Marty... hell, you know Marty.

"Moe, Larry, Curly... move it," I said, jerking my thumb to the side. They backed away from the dingus. I walked over, got my arms mostly wrapped around it, and, surprising myself, picked the damn thing up. It had to be made of aluminum. It weighed about as much as a sack and a half of cement. Maybe it wasn't a bomb, but I didn't want to take any chances leaving it next to a roaring fire. I ended up setting it down on its side and rolling it. Marty, Art and Les pitched in and we got it about ten yards away from the fire and away from the shore. "We need to hide this thing. It's dangerous."

"Dangerous? How?" Art asked.

"If I'm right, it could vaporize this island."

"That doesn't sound good at all," Marty said. "And me just married."

"I told you we aren't married, you dope!" Dottie said, standing behind us. She smacked him on the side of the head.

"I'm pretty sure—"

"—we aren't! You have to *wash* the gal's feet, not *rub* them, in order to be married. Good job by the way. First class foot rub. May let you do it again if you behave yourself."

"Yes, ma'am!"

"So this... thing?" Dottie asked me. "It could explode?"

"It may be a bomb. A big bomb."

Dottie studied the problem. She walked around the atomic dingus, nudged it a little with her foot, got down and rolled it back and forth. "It's a lot lighter than it looks," she said. "We could make a stretcher with the two poles Heena and Judy were tied to and some of that rope and carry it out into the jungle, stash it somewhere. Sandy, Ruby and I could handle that. Easy-peasy. That would leave you free to thrash these idiots within an inch of their lives. I'd hate to have to punch their lights out. Just did my nails." She held out her hands so we could inspect.

Marty leaned over and licked her hand. She boxed his ears and he fell to the ground, moaning, "Why? Why?"

"They have no respect for a classy dame like myself. None whatsoever."

"I'd like to lick your hand, but I have too much respect for you," Art said.

"I, too, have a lot of respect for you," Les said. They both attempted winning smiles.

Marty struggled to his feet. "My ears are ringing. Is my nose bleeding? Take a look at my nose. Is it bleeding? Why aren't you talking? Am I deaf now?"

Ruby walked over and waved a can at the three hapless men. "Hey! Where'd you get the can of... what is this stuff? Patty?"

"May I?" She handed me the can. "Pâté de foie de canard," I read off the can. "It's French. Goop made from duck livers. Goes on crackers. Did you get this directly from the French, or did you jokers find the French ship?"

"Ah, so we know something you don't know!" Art declared. "The advantage is ours!"

"Yes, yes!" Les concurred. "We shall have sex with these damsels—"

But before either of them could get another word out, Dottie grabbed the hair on the backs of their heads and bashed them together forehead to forehead. The sound was like a cantaloupe falling onto a grocery store floor. Clean-up in aisle three! She let go and they fell down, taking Marty with them, all three groaning on the black sand, rolling around dramatically.

"This is a lot of pain!" Art said.

"My head!" Les said.

"You were saying?" Dottie went, glaring down at them. She wiped her hands on her grass skirt.

"She touched me," Art said to Marty.

"I touched her first, though," Marty said to Art.

"Mondo help me!" Dottie said. The volcano rumbled unhelpfully.

Art looked up at her. "Technically, it's 'Maui help me.' As in 'Maui-Tiki-Tiki-A-Taranga,' which is the actual name of the god of the—ow! Stop kicking me!"

I stepped in between her and the wounded men, who seemed to be enjoying the rough treatment a little too much.

Marty said, "Her papa never got the name right!"

"Please let me kill them, beefcake. I swear, I'll only kill them a little."

"Dottie, cool off. I'll handle this."

She tossed up her hands. "Fine. Keep them away from me." She stalked off about 12 yards and sat on a rock, leaning forward, elbows on knees.

"Hey, Ruby!" Art said, righting himself.

"Ugh," Ruby went, and walked back over to the fruit pile.

"Take a knee," I said to the three lads. They watched me do it, and knelt down in a circle around me. "You want to impress those gals?"

"You know we do, big guy," Art said.

"What would he know about impressing a girl?" Les asked. "All that he has to do is strut into a room and the dames fall all over him."

"Don't be a fathead. Shut your yaps and listen to me."

"Yes, sir!" the three chimed together.

"If you guys show us out to the French boat, I'm sure you doll-dizzy dimwits could get lucky. Or luckier than you have so far. Dames like a fella who takes risks. A fella who is a provider."

"Give us a moment, will you?" Art asked.

I got up and walked over to Dottie. "What's the plan?" Dottie asked.

"You may have to get more foot rubs," I said.

"As long as it's just a foot rub," Dottie said, peering around me at the lads.

"Who knows? Those three could surprise you." I fished around in my pockets looking for a pack of smokes. I found my leftover cigar and lit it with the Zippo.

"I doubt it."

"I figure you could execute your plan to hide the dingus, and I could take Heena with me to the boat." I twisted the cigar in my mouth, letting the good tobacco nestle its way down my larynx.

"Take Judy, too. She's a hell of a swimmer."

Dottie stood up and stretched her arms above her. She was a magnificent woman. She had unblemished dark brown skin, was muscular with an athlete's poise, grace and symmetry. Her black hair fell in waves across her chest and back halfway down to her waist. She had wide-set, almond-shaped eyes with wheat-colored irises that sparkled with intelligence, a pointed nose, ripe pink lips and perfect rows of large white teeth. If General Mills put her on a cereal box, that cereal would sell out in a day. Girls would it eat wanting to be her, and men would ogle the box. Back home, our society would take an incredible woman like her and try to shove her into a kitchen. Given the color of her skin, she'd be wearing a maid's outfit. I imagined her in a maid's uniform, and then had to get the hell away from her before I got an erection. "Will do," I said.

I walked back to the lads.

"We'll do it, big guy!" Art announced. "For sex! Or love! One of those."

"There's the kind of decisiveness that can make a man attractive to the fairer sex," I said. I took one last puff and chucked the cigar into the surf. "We're going to take Heena and Judy with us. Dottie, Sandy and Ruby are going to take the atomic dingus somewhere safe. I'm betting there are enough stores on board that ship to last a few months. Cheese, wine, cans of this goop." I pitched the can over and it landed in the pile of food. "Cigarettes, too."

"This is the sort of thing that could reunite our tribes," Marty said. "Gloria!"

"We could all get married!" Les said. "Irene!"

"Louise!" Art said.

"Louise?" Marty said. "Seriously? Louise?"

"Aw, she's so darned cute."

"Hard to argue with that."

"I'd tickle her and make her giggle."

"The laughter of girls!"

"As long as they're not laughing *at* you, it's like music!"

I started feeling badly for these out-of-shape weirdos. They just needed someone to teach them how to be men, I told myself unconvincingly. "Can the chatter and let's get a move-on," I said, clapping my hands.

Journey to Mount Taranga!

Heena, Ruby and Sandy, having sated themselves on the pile of food, made a little skirt out of palm fronds for Judy. It wasn't as nice as the ones Dottie, Ruby and Sandy had on, but it would do in a pinch. It was green and didn't cover much up. Heena, meanwhile, had tied my shirt around her waist. "My nipples were getting sore," she said by way of explanation.

I leaned in and kissed her lasciviously, and she leaned into it. After we finished kissing, I whispered in her ear, "The things I'm going to do to you when we get back home…" I realized that I meant the hut, not the States. I'd been here less than a week, and now I couldn't imagine being anywhere else.

"Bay-bees!" she whispered back breathlessly.

"Beautiful babies."

Judy stood there smiling, her hands clasped together under her chin. It was the first smile I'd seen from her.

"It's good to see you smile, Judy," I said.

"It's good to see my sister happy," she said, and those were the first words I'd ever witnessed emerging from her mouth. "You're going to stay after the Americans come?"

"Of course I am. None of these boys appeal to you?"

"No," she said. "I wish they did. But no. There's a jungle soldier I like, but I don't think he even looks at me. His name is Toshiro. He's brave and sweet."

"I won't let anything like this happen again."

"Don't worry about it. We can take care of ourselves." She nodded toward her much larger sisters, who were rigging up the atomic dingus to the poles for carrying, while the lads lingered around them, watching them. Heena's arm worked its way around my waist and my arm draped naturally across her shoulders.

"We should all get a little shut-eye," I said. "Where do you lads sleep?"

"Here on the beach," Les said.

"Sometimes in a cave over on Mount Taranga," and he pointed to a black hill about a quarter of a mile away, partially hidden by foliage.

"You mean Mount Tonya?" Heena asked.

"Did your pop get anything right about our culture? Even one little bit?" Art let his irritation seep through.

Heena and Judy let it go with a patronizing rolling of the eyes.

"Let me talk to Dottie for a second," I said. I walked over to her. They'd finished the rig. We discussed it for a moment and decided that the lads would sleep on the beach, while Dottie, Sandy, Ruby, Heena, Judy and I would go up to the cave. Dottie, Sandy and Ruby would get up before dawn, take the dingus somewhere else to hide it—Dottie said she knew a place—and then the three big gals would head back to the village.

My team, which would include the three lads I'd chosen, would lug as much stuff off the French ship as we could carry back to the village.

I returned to my team and told them the plan.

"Can we come with you to the cave tonight?" Art asked. "Just us chosen three?"

"No," I said. "As you can well imagine, Dottie has lost any trust she used to have in you. So cool your heels here until first light."

"Ah, applesauce!" Marty went. I suppose if I'd been taught English by missionaries from Pennsylvania, I'd talk like that, too. I was willing to bet that Marty had never even tasted applesauce, much less an apple.

"Don't snap your cap," I said. "Just go with the plan. Remember what I told you."

"Irene!" Les said, like a prayer.

Someone Walked Over My Grave!

Ruby volunteered to scout ahead. She leapt off through the narrow jungle path like a panther, her short hair, bobbed and banged like a flapper, swaying as she disappeared up ahead.

I stuck close to Heena, not wanting to let her out of my sight for a moment. As the path narrowed and darkened, she slipped ahead of me, but I kept a hand on her shoulder. She was warm and soft.

The foliage overhead blocked out the night stars, so I lost my sense of direction as the path twisted and turned. I could tell we were going up and up. I lost my foothold at one point and slipped, but Heena turned around quickly and grasped my elbow with one hand and my wrist with the other and pulled me back up. "Don't fall," she said.

"Sound advice."

Sandy was right behind us. "You're too slow. Speed

up!"

I turned around and saw that Judy was riding on the dingus like it was a mule, as Sandy carried from the front and Dottie carried from the rear. Sandy wasn't even winded. I peered back at Dottie, who said, "Quit your lollygagging!"

"You heard the lady," I said to Heena, and she sped right up.

In about a half hour, we made it to the cave, a ten-foot-high by five-foot-wide recess carved by nature into a pile of igneous rock. The jungle quieted down and we paused by the entrance, only to see one of the jungle soldiers come leaping out, pulling up his pants.

"Yankee Doodle!" he shouted at me, almost accusingly, and dashed hatless down a path opposite us.

Ruby sauntered out of the cave, licking her bottom lip absently, and fluffing the back of her hair with the tips of her fingers, her breasts bobbing and nipples hard.

"The jungle soldier again?" Heena asked.

"What? Hiro? You had sexy time with him once or twice," Ruby said. "He's cute. I taught him the tongue kissing you told me about. He seemed to enjoy it. Then he got too grabby and I had to give him a couple of whacks on the behind."

"Bet he enjoyed that even more," I said.

"You're kind of judgy, beefcake," Dottie said, as she and Sandy carried the atomic dingus past, with Judy sitting upon it, swinging her tiny sleek legs, looking up into the trees and smiling slyly as if at a joke she'd told herself. They took it into the cave and set it down, and then came back out. Dottie stretched her arms out and then sat down with her legs together and straight ahead of her and reached for her toes.

They talked about when their Aunt Flo would arrive, which was, they agreed, a couple of weeks away. As they talked, they automatically gathered wood and cleared an area for a fire. They were synchronized in every way. It was mesmerizing to watch.

I stood there like a lump. A useless lump. They barely noticed me until they sat down around the fire, sipping water out of what looked like Coca-Cola bottles. "Cop a squat, beefcake," Dottie said, patting the ground between her and Heena. "Take a load off."

I sat down and watched the show on the other side of the fire, Sandy and Ruby braiding Judy's hair. Sandy reached down and tickled Judy's ribs a little and Judy sat up and giggled, turned around and slapped at her half-heartedly. "See, she *does* smile," Sandy said.

"Who knew?" Ruby said.

Heena reached over and took my hand. "What's the

matter, Russo?"

"What do you mean?"

"You look like someone walked over your grave," Dottie said.

How could I explain it to them? How could I say that the only other time I felt this close to a group of people was back in the Army? And that on December 13, 1944, I watched every one of those men die? I remember the kamikaze heading for the landing ship I was on. I remember being thrown from the force of its impact and then...

After that, I volunteered for every shitty mission.

I should hate the jungle soldiers, I thought. Why didn't I hate them? Only a decade before, I would have, without hesitation, without provocation, killed every one of them. Was that man, that me, just a temporary version who was quickly shelved after the war ended? Who was that man? I don't know. I was glad he wasn't around, not at that moment anyway. I wanted him to stay on a shelf, shoved in a cold, dark basement deep inside. He was quiet on that shelf.

I thought of Hiro, stuck on this island for a decade as a soldier with no orders. Or maybe his orders were to kill himself rather than be taken prisoner. To resist unto death. I thought of the flamethrowers we used when the Japanese troops wouldn't come out of their hideyholes. I remembered how they resisted at Fort Drum, a concrete permanent emplacement like a stationary battleship in Manila harbor, and how we had to pour diesel fuel and set the thing on fire to drive them out. Their screams.

I remembered how emaciated they were. I remembered how I had no pity for them at the time, and then when I was in the hospital, I could not stop seeing them. Sitting there at the fire with those bright and chipper gals, those men I killed appeared to me, just for an instant, and then I forcefully shoved the memory away.

The Japanese were misguided and misled.

The jungle soldiers should be given the opportunity to go home just like I was given that opportunity. Everyone should get to go home, even if they decide to leave it again. Like I did.

I don't know. I was a soldier once. That's all I know.

I forced myself to smile at the girls. "We should have marshmallows to roast," I said. "That would make this perfect."

"Marshmallows?" Heena said. "What funny things you say!" She kissed me on the cheek. She stroked my cheek with the knuckle-side of her fingers. "I need to shave you again."

I saw Judy staring at me, through the flames, as if she

was reading my mind, as if she saw for an instant all of the horrible things I'd done. *It wasn't me!* I wanted to say. I have that guy locked up! She shook her head and the braids came loose, and Sandy and Ruby started in on her hair again.

"You two treat her like she's your doll because she's small," Dottie said. She pulled a foot up to her hip and manually pulled and cracked her toes.

I turned and looked at Heena and her face, that beautiful face, softened. "I love you, Heena," I said.

"We'll make beautiful babies together," she said, her celestial eyes glowing. "They'll make you happy with all the life inside them."

I hoped she was right.

Ship of the Damned!

I awoke in a heap of girls. The last embers of the fire flickered out and the first light of dawn heated the jungle, which coughed, sputtered and started up its wild cackling and cawing. In front of me was Dottie, whose face had turned innocent in her sleep, her muscular forearms flattened together and her hands palm-to-palm cushioning her bronzed cheek. I could feel Heena behind me, her face pressed between my shoulder blades. I sat up, which awakened Heena, and saw Judy squished between Sandy and Ruby. Judy awoke, squirmed her way out from between them, and gave each of them a good shake. Judy's expression changed the moment she awoke, from relaxed to cynical. She peered around skeptically, and then bounded into the jungle, returning with some fruit.

"You get to carry that dingus today," Sandy said to Ruby.

"Shouldn't be too far," Dottie said, stretching. "Then we can go to the spring for a good soak."

Heena sprinted up a coconut tree and returned with three. She expertly bashed them against the mouth of the cave and they opened right up. She handed them to Dottie, Ruby and Sandy.

"Where are those three jugheads?" I wondered aloud.

As if on cue, the three lads came puffing out of the jungle, sat down heavily and expressed their dismay at the long uphill walk. Judy immediately scooted between Sandy and Ruby, and Ruby placed a protective hand on her back.

All the girls glared over at Art, Les and Marty scoldingly.

"We're sorry!" Art said. "How many times do we have to say that?"

"Keep saying it," Dottie said. "We'll let you know when it's enough."

We all ate silently as the gals eyeballed the men angrily, and the men eyeballed the girls hungrily.

After breakfast, we quickly broke up into two groups. Dottie and Ruby picked up the atomic dingus, with Sandy pulling up the rear, and they disappeared into the jungle, but not before Dottie said to me confidentially, "Keep an eye on those three. They seem more skittish than usual."

"Aye, ma'am," I replied.

We followed Art, Les and Marty down the same path that Hiro had walked down. There was no lovey-dovey between me and the missus, as Judy inserted herself between us. Soon, we found ourselves in a small cove, and there, trapped on a reef, was the wrecked French freighter, ever-so-slightly listing to port.

"There it is," Marty said, waving at it.

"Can we go now?" Les asked.

"What's the rush?" Heena asked.

"Ah... I don't like being here," Les said.

"Long walk back to camp," Art said. "Let's get going."

"Yes, let's go," Les said.

"We are in agreement," Marty said.

"Suit yourselves," Heena said, and then took my shirt off and tossed it on the beach. Judy did likewise with her new skirt. The two nude women waded out into the cove, dunked themselves and emerged from the water, the early morning sun making their skin glisten like precious metal.

The three lads stood there for a moment gawking, and then Art snapped out of it first and poked the other two. They backed into another trail, stumbling over each other and exposed roots, rocks and bushes.

"See you later!" Art called out.

"It's not like they hadn't seen us nude before," Judy said. She splashed more water on her face, and then floated on her back, stroking the water with her arms and fluttering her tiny feet.

I stripped down to my BVDs, throwing my Dodgers hat, khakis, boots, t-shirt and socks on top of my shirt and Judy's new skirt and waded in.

"He's so muscly," Judy said to Heena.

"I know! You should see his pa-tang-tang!"

"Irene told me about it."

The two women giggled musically, while I blushed.

"Okay, enough horsing around. Let's get out to that ship," I said.

"Aw, Russo! Don't be sore," Heena said. She waded over to me and kissed me on the lips, her hands tickling the back of my neck, her tongue dancing momentarily between my lips. "We'll make sexy time later."

Judy was already heading out to the ship, swimming like a porpoise, doing the breaststroke. She was a fast swimmer and quickly made it there. By the time we started swimming, she was already climbing a rope ladder and waving to us.

We swam out to the ship and Heena climbed the ladder first, and I enjoyed the view on the way up.

The deck of the ship was teak. I saw Judy's dainty footprints leading to a watertight door. I opened the door, and there greeting us was Judy, her hands behind her back, her ankles bound by rope, standing under a glowing bare light bulb recessed in the overhead. Leaning against the bulkhead was a tall, elegantly dressed SS officer, complete with monocle, jackboots, saucer hat with a skull and bones, gray-black uniform adorned with a single Iron Cross, a riding crop under one arm and a Luger in his opposite hand.

"Herr Russo!" he said in a clipped English accent. "How *kind* of you to join us!"

A band of a half-dozen scruffy Japanese soldiers stood around, toting their empty rifles, rusty bayonets attached. They looked vaguely excited and slightly bored. Most of their attention was on the two nude gals.

"Well, if it isn't a real, live Nazi," I said. "Haven't had the pleasure."

"How rude of me! My name is Oberleutnant Otto von Schlechteren. I'm a special advisor to the Japanese Imperial Army."

"I have news for you, you Kraut shithead. The war is over!"

"Yes, of course you would say that. I suppose the Americans won? How ridiculous! Seize him!"

One of the soldiers walked over to me, smiling apologetically, and expertly butt-stroked me across the jaw.

Hellcat, Baby!

I awoke tied to a chair, covered in water, looking into the disinterested face of a jug-eared soldier in a tatty uniform with an empty tin pail in his hands, his unloaded rifle cross-slung on his back. His eyes were jaundiced with malaria, his teeth blackened. I was under the dim lightbulb, my head pounding. I opened my mouth experimentally, stretching my jaw. That soldier had clocked me good.

I blinked and looked around. This was supposed to be a recreation room, I guessed. Maybe, once upon a time, it had a certain charm, but not anymore. It was the kind of room that cried out for plush furniture and fake rubber tree plants, for subdued paint, and deep carpeting, but instead was garish, with glass bricks allowing some light in from the outside. The flat carpet was patterned like water bugs floating in a swimming pool that hadn't seen chlorine in a year or two. The bulkheads looked like they'd been soaked in grape Nehi, and were covered over in black and white photos of the ship at sea, as if you'd need to know what that looked like while you were aboard that very same ship at sea. The acoustic tile overhead was blotched over in yellow stains. Maybe the monkeys had redecorated the joint. Or a lunatic.

Heena and Judy were bound hand and foot, sitting in a

corner to my right, hands resting on their drawn-up knees, their backs against the bulkhead. Both gals looked more than a little peeved.

My hands were tied behind my back, my legs each tied to a chair leg. I gave my arms a little tug. The ropes bit into me. The Nazi walked over and placed his hands on my knees, leaning into my face. I could smell his breath—surprisingly, it was like lilacs—and could see my reflection in his monocle. I had a purple bruise on my jaw. "We have ways of making you talk," the Nazi said.

"I've heard that one before," I said.

The German gritted his teeth tightly. His jawline went white. His blue eyes narrowed. I heard his breath whistle through his nose. "Where is this... what do you call it? Atomic dingus? Yes! Where is this object? Hmm? Please answer me, Herr Russo. Where is the dingus?" He stood up straight and strutted around the room, slapping the riding crop against his leg. He handed the riding crop to one of his Japanese lackeys and pulled a small dagger from a sheath attached to his belt, stuck the point of the blade inside my nostril, gave it a small yank, and I felt a shot of pain go right through me. Blood spurted onto my lap. I could feel it, warm and damp across my knees.

"The war is over," I said, speaking to the room. "You should all go home to your families. I'm sure they're worried about you."

"Ah, hah-hah!" the Oberleutnant went. A tight smile struggled its way across his face. "Yes, so you have said before. We, none of us, believe you, of course."

"Who won?" one of the soldiers asked. I squinted through the dim light. It was Hiro.

"Jesus, Hiro! What are you doing with this guy?"

"I am a soldier. It is my duty."

"The war's over. You should be settling down with Ruby, having kids, not playing around with this Nazi nitwit."

"I have my orders," Hiro said. "My duty. My honor."

"Japan is doing great. You make these nifty transistor radios and little motorcycles. Everyone is happy there now that the war's over."

"Who won?" Hiro asked again.

"Um... you guys did."

Hiro turned around and said it in Japanese, which elicited a cheer.

"So Germany was victorious as well?" the Nazi asked.

"Oh, uh... they tried to build something called an 'atom bomb' and accidentally blew themselves up."

Hiro turned around and translated that bit of news to the other Japanese, who glared at the Nazi unsympathetically.

"Mein Gott," von Schlechteren said, turning around to the Japanese. "This man is clearly a liar."

"Why would he lie about losing the war?" Hiro asked.

"We all have a common enemy now," I said, going for broke. "The Russians."

"*That* I can believe," the Nazi said. "Nonetheless, I must ask you again for the location of the atomic dingus. I must have this object."

"Give it a rest," I said. I wriggled my nose. The blood was already coagulating into a scab.

"We'll see how smart you are when I cut off *die Rute*," he said. He brandished his dagger and then used it to cut off my BVDs, which he pulled off me and tossed aside. They all stood staring at my cock as I rolled my eyes in embarrassment. "My compliments, Herr Russo. Truly. And uh, I thought I was the only one who shaved in such a manner."

Hiro translated and the Japanese all laughed.

"Purely for hygiene purposes!" von Schlechteren said. "I mean... am I not correct, Herr Russo? Hygiene?" He continued staring at my penis. He crouched down and touched it with the tip of his index finger. "It is impressive. It shall look more impressive after I cut it off and place it in a box in my quarters!"

While none of us were paying attention, Heena, growing increasingly enraged, untied her feet. We did notice when she leapt upon von Schlechteren suddenly from behind with a shrill war-cry, her arms around his throat, choking him with the rope still tied to her wrists. The Nazi dropped the dagger onto the deck and reached up to the rope that my angry lady had wrapped around his neck. "Nobody touches my man's pa-tang-tang but me!" she shouted.

The Nazi couldn't speak. He stood up straight, and Heena tightened her death hold on him. His eyes bulged and his face grew pale. She growled like a panther.

The Japanese spectated, undecided on what they should do next.

"Kill him, Heena! Kill him good!" Judy shouted.

The Nazi passed out and Heena let him drop to the deck with a loud thud. His monocle rolled across the floor on its side like a dropped quarter taking a hike on a city sidewalk. She spat on him. His high-peaked hat had skittered across the room somewhere. She turned to Hiro. "Well?"

"Hellcat, baby!" he said appreciatively. He placed his

rifle on the deck and picked up the dagger. He cut the rope on her hands and cut me loose quickly.

Pretty Judy!

"Did you Tojos already pilfer everything in this bucket?" I asked Hiro.

"Wha—?"

"Are there any stores left on board?"

"Oh! I, um—"

"Stop staring at my pa-tang-tang."

"It is difficult not to look, Russo-san."

I crossed my legs and put my hands on top of it. "All right. Answer my question."

"There is much cargo still in this ship," he said.

"I'm hoping for a pair of pants myself," I muttered.

"Do me a favor and tie the German up."

"Of course." He barked out orders to the Japanese. They snapped to attention and then fell out, and gathered up rope.

One of the jungle soldiers untied Judy, and she slapped him. The tears started pouring out of her. Kidnapped twice in two days. Not a good feeling. The jungle soldier turned his head from her in shame, a hand over the slapped area. Then Judy reached over and hugged him. "Judy," he said to her. "Judy, Judy."

Heena stood over von Schlechteren, very gravely watching him get tied up. I unholstered his luger. I had nowhere to put it, being naked myself, and placed it on the chair. She fell into my arms and began to cry. "I could have killed him," she said, weeping and sniffling against my chest.

"Shh, shh," I went.

"He shouldn't have—"

"Hush now." I held her against me and let her cry.

Soon enough, Hiro stood at attention next to us. He waved a pair of bell-bottomed dungarees, a pair of fancy skivvies and a blue-and-white striped, wide-necked sailor's jumper at me. He found a pair of suede penny loafers to go along with it. "Thanks, Hiro," I said. He smiled, clicked his heels and bowed. I put it all on quickly. "I'm willing to bet I look ridiculous."

"You look… gorgeous," Heena said. She got up on her tip-toes and kissed me carefully.

"We could find something for you to wear. Possibly the latest fashion from Paris."

"I'm fine," she said. "I'll put your shirt back on when we get to shore."

"But you're all naked, sweetheart."

She beamed, and did a little twirl for me, bit her lip winningly. "Gosh darn it, had no idea! So I am." She was a pin-up girl come to life. She had no shame about her body. None whatsoever. She didn't care if anyone saw her in her birthday suit. My parish priest would have been horrified, but I wasn't. She was perfect in mind, body and spirit.

Judy pranced over, also still nude, holding her soldier's hand, dragging the sheepish man to meet us. "This is Toshiro," she said.

Toshiro looked up at us, bowed, kind of made a gesture with his eyebrows, and said, "I like Judy. She is pretty."

"I bet that's most of the English you know," I said.

"She is pretty," he replied. "Pretty Judy."

A woman can make a man so much better than he has any right to be. I've never known the inverse to be true. We men have a lot of catching up to do.

Galloping Ghost!

The good Oberleutnant awoke, hacking, and realized he was tied up. His eyes locked on me.

"Let me guess: 'You'll pay for this, Herr Russo! If it is the last thing I do, you shall pay for this.'" I shook my fist at him mockingly.

"You look ridiculous in that French ponce's outfit," he said, his voice roughened by his recent strangling.

I walked over to his monocle where it still lay on the floor and crushed it under my heel. "You were saying?"

He sighed, which came out almost like a gurgle. "Is the war really over?"

"It's over. It was bad at the end for your side. Germany

is split in half now."

"I was... rash before. I apologize for my ill manners."

"I wasn't kidding about the Russians. The U.S., Japan and West Germany are allies in the free world now against the communists. The Reds are probably heading this way."

I picked up the Luger from the chair and carefully placed it on the deck. I hoisted the German up by his armpits, situating him on the chair. He was trussed up like a pork roast ready to go into the oven. I picked up the Luger again and sniffed it. It was well oiled, but hadn't been fired recently. "You got any rounds left in this popgun, Otto?"

"One," he said. "I was saving it for when the despair became too much."

"Hang on, Herr Oberleutnant. You'll be going home soon enough if my people make it here first." I shoved the Luger in the back of my dungarees. "Unless you had something to do with concentration camps. Then you get to visit sunny Israel."

"Israel!"

"Yeah. The surviving European Jews aren't too happy with your kind. If you're a rocket scientist, however, we're hiring."

"You would not happen to have any cigarettes, Herr Russo?"

"Sorry. All out. I'm willing to bet there are a ton of them in the cargo hold. I mean, it *is* a French ship."

"And wine!"

"And wine. Don't go anywhere." I slapped him playfully on the cheek. "Heena and I are gonna take a looky-loo downstairs."

"Are you going to leave me tied up like this?"

"You did threaten to cut off my cock, if you recall. I think a cooling-off period is in order."

"Right. Of course you're right." I found his cover in the corner and placed it on his head at a rakish angle.

Judy had slipped behind Toshiro, I noticed.

"Judy, pretty Judy," Toshiro said, as her little arms wrapped around him and gave him a squeeze.

"Keep it up, Toshiro. I think you're winning her over."

"Notre Dame! Knute Rockne," he said, full of bonhomie. "Four horsemen."

"Judy, make sure our German friend stays seated. Have Toshiro give him a poke with his bayonet if he doesn't."

"I assure you I will not attempt to move, mein freund."

Judy slipped out from behind Toshiro. "I'll keep an eye on him, Russo. Don't you worry."

I leaned in and whispered, "Get her some flowers, Toshiro. A bouquet."

"Red Grange," he whispered in return, confidentially. "Galloping ghost." He winked at me, and slapped me on the bicep. We were two men with beautiful women on our arms. We had the world by the ass and we knew it.

Hot Lust of the Altered Apes!

Heena and I found the radio room first during our wanderings through the ship. I was hoping that I could establish comms with Seventh Fleet. But we found that the radio had been destroyed almost completely. I opened the watertight door and found bloody handprints on the bulkheads, wires ripped out of the radio, smashed vacuum tubes, and a handset and headphones on the deck, bits of blood and hair on each, the chair tilted on its side.

Heena slipped behind me. On this island, she hadn't been subjected to anything like the barbarity that regularly occurs in the outside world. I grew up on the southside of Chicago, so I'd seen such things often in my youth. And the Army took me to places that were beyond sanity. That said, the bloody scene made even me queasy. It was a fearsome sight.

"Somebody didn't like old Sparky," I said. "That much is clear."

There was no body in the room, though I could see where he'd been dragged to the door.

"Let's get out of here, Russo." I turned around and she had her eyes closed tightly. I leaned down, grasped her bottom and lifted her up in the radio room and set her down in the passageway so she wouldn't trip, and I closed the watertight door behind us.

"That's it, keep your eyes closed. Shove it away. Shove it away quickly and do your best to forget you saw it." I took her a few yards down the passageway. "Open your eyes and look at me." She did so. What I saw there was all too familiar. I'd seen it in a lot of faces during the war—that initial horror shock. "Everything's going to be okay. Breathe in, breathe out. Attagirl. You're doing great." I took her in my arms and caressed her back, from her delicate neck down to her tailbone. "Shh. Shh."

We found the passenger cabins and strolled through the deck arm-in-arm. She still had the shakes. The wood-paneled passageway was covered over in framed pastels of seascapes, as if none of the passengers could peer out the portholes and see the sea. The passengers were not there in body, but they were eerily present as we went through their rooms one-by-one. I opened drawers and found them filled with clothes, socks, skivvies, lighters, cigarettes, condoms. French-language newspapers littered decks and surfaces. Stubbed out cigarettes, some tipped in lipstick, filled ashtrays advertising Cinzano.

Heena peered around my shoulder as I pawed through the remains of the passengers' lives. I found a small spray bottle of Chanel No. 5 in a cabin that had been occupied by a tasteful woman. I uncapped the bottle and sniffed it. I held it out for Heena. She took a whiff.

"Oh, that's pretty, Russo!"

I sprayed a dab on my index finger and ran my finger from collarbone to collarbone, across her lovely throat. I kissed the rope burns on her wrists. Even though the ship was listing slightly, I could imagine the two of us aboard her at sea on a romantic holiday, maybe our honeymoon. We stood staring into each other's eyes, lapsing into a mutual fugue for a long time before we kissed.

When we finished, "Russo…" she whispered in my ear, and let it trail off. She lightly stroked the bruise on my chin.

"Let's see if this dame had any clothes that would fit you. I think it would be fun to dress you up." I figured it might help to take her mind off what she'd just seen in the radio room. I pulled the Kraut peashooter out of my waistband and set it on the dresser.

She tilted her head and grinned. I walked over to the closet and opened it up. I found a sun dress with a white hibiscus print on royal blue. In a drawer I found panties, and silk stockings with a garter belt. In a closet, I found a shoe box containing a pair of black suede pumps with black bows on the front. She had no trouble slipping on the panties. I had to show her how to put on the stockings with the garters—I'd watched Geri do it enough times. I helped her put on the dress and zipped her up. It all fit her perfectly. She wobbled in the shoes, attempting to walk around, and kept fidgeting with her panties and the garter belt under the dress. Finally, she patted down the dress and stood still for a moment. I sat down on the bed and drank her in.

"For future reference, you're a perfect size 12," I told her. "Absolutely perfect. By God, you have class. Buckets of class!"

She beamed at that. "All of this feels so strange." She navigated her way to the bed and fell next to me. "How do your women walk in these?"

"Beats me. You should see the way your legs look in those stockings and pumps though. Mercy!"

She sat up on the bed, dangling her million dollar gams over the side, only her toes in the shoes now. I got up and found the lady's makeup kit and brought it over, popping it open. I found a particularly red shade of lipstick and painted a streak on her lower lip.

"Rub your lips together, like this," and I demonstrated. She did so. I made her close her eyes and dabbed on some blue eye shadow. I put some rouge on her cheeks. It was an inexpert job, though I'd watched Geri do it dozens of times. When I asked her to reopen her eyes, I held a little compact mirror for her to peer into.

"Oh my!" she said, snatching the mirror from my hand. "Oh, is this me?" She vamped a bit for the mirror, turning her head from side to side, making faces, fluffing her hair, puckering her lips. "Is this what the women in Chicago look like?"

"No, sweetheart," I said. "None of them could hold a candle to you."

Pretty soon, all of our newly acquired clothes were on the deck, and we were ensconced in the sheets in a most athletic way for the next hour or so.

Give or take. Island time.

Civilization!

Much to my surprise and delight, Heena decided to put the dress back on. She didn't put on the rest of the stuff. The shoes were confusing to a woman who'd never worn a pair, and the panties and other garments felt strange and uncomfortable to her. The dress fit her snugly in all the right places.

In the bathroom, I found some facial tissue and wiped all the lipstick off me. I pulled on my adopted clothes, shoved the luger back in my waistband. In a drawer underneath, I found a hairbrush. "Come here," I said, waving her back over to the bed. I sat behind her and brushed her long, wavy black hair, and it shined. It was late afternoon now. The world outside the porthole was turning golden.

She picked up the cosmetics case and rummaged through it as I continued brushing her hair. She found false eyelashes and dropped them, thinking they were bugs. She found cremes and an entire palette of varying shades of face paint, an eyelash trimmer, horsehair brushes, and a powderpuff. She opened containers and sniffed their contents. She opened up tubes of lipstick, and twisted them out.

"Maybe we should find some food now, Russo," she said, closing the case and setting it aside.

I put down the hair brush and held her from behind for a moment, taking in the scent of her and her warmth. "Yes," I said. "I'm good and hungry now." There came a realization that I would take a bullet for this woman, that I would do anything to see her smile. A week ago, neither of us knew the other existed.

She slid off the bed and stood up, and I quickly stood up behind her. I swept her hair aside and kissed her gently on the neck. "I love the way you touch me," she said.

"You're fun to touch, sweetheart." I caressed her some more. I lifted her dress above her hips and caressed her lovely bottom.

She gasped. "Stop, stop, stop," and she gently swatted my hands away.

I gave her a quick smooch and then we left the ghost woman's cabin. We found a ladder and went down into the cargo hold, and what we experienced there stopped us both in our tracks.

First, it was the smell. It was feces, urine, wet straw. It was fear. It was blood scent, like spoiled meat. The cages were empty, but you could see how the primates had been forced to live. We walked through the hold, barely breathing. "Good God!" I said at last.

"Civilization," Heena said, seething with contempt.

There was blood on one wall, spattered, and there was something more within the spatters. There was a stainless steel surgical table with an electric saw, a dremel, a hand-cranked drill, wires, and more blood and more matter, that I could only assume was brains. There were bunsen burners and test tubes lined up in wooden racks. There was a peg board where I could make out, in the blood spray, the outlines of several tools that were missing. There were a dozen of the monkey helmets scattered on the floor out of an overturned box.

"Let's get out of here," I said.

"Those poor monkeys," Heena said, her voice muffled, her hand over her mouth. She stepped on a screw, and hopped on one foot. She steadied herself holding onto my shoulder and turned her injured foot toward me. I took the screw out. A little blood came with it. I picked her up and carried her over to a chair, dug around in a fireproof box and found a first aid kit. I poured hydrogen peroxide on her wound, it fizzed a bit, and then put some gauze on her and wrapped her foot and the gauze with most of a roll of adhesive tape. I put more bandages in one pocket and the tape in the other.

"Hop on my back," I said, turning around.

"I can walk."

"You'll get an infection from the floor. Look at this place."

She wrapped her arms around my neck and wrapped her feet around my waist, and I carried her up the ladder like that.

I'd seen men lose limbs in the tropics with wounds smaller than hers. I immediately started obsessing. I'd want to look at the wound as soon as I could after a few hours.

We'd emerged on a different deck. The ship was a maze. Heena hopped off my back and limped a bit down the passageway. I opened a waterproof door, and stood staring at enough canned goods to last our village a year. One enormous can was labeled "Ragoût de Bœuf" and another "Minuscules Carottes dans le Vin." A wooden crate was labeled, "Vin Pétillant." I popped that one open, and pulled out a bottle of Pinot Noir Crémant d'Alsace Rosé, 1952.

I took the can of stew, the tiny carrots, and the bottle of fizzy wine into the galley, which was right next door. The galley kitchen was tiny. I opened the big can with a hand-cranked can opener, bolted onto a clean stainless steel table with a vice. I dunked my finger in the stew and placed it in Heena's mouth. She sucked as I pulled my finger from her lips. "What is that?" she asked, smacking her lips.

"It's beef stew."

"It's strange."

"Your father is going to be thrilled. This is the closest thing he's liable to find to that steak he asked me about."

"I don't know if I like it." She smacked her tongue around. "Strange aftertaste."

I opened the can of tiny carrots, and fed her one.

"I like that. That's good."

I found a corkscrew in a drawer under the table and opened the sparkling wine with a loud pop. Heena yelped and leapt backwards, and laughed. The wine fizzed over the top. I handed it to her and she sipped and coughed. It smelled like strawberries.

The stove still had gas. I found a match and lit it, dumping the stew into a pan. I lit another burner and put the carrots into a smaller pan. I found plates above the stove and wine glasses in a cabinet next to those. I poured her a glass of wine. "Sip it slowly," I said.

She sucked it right down and shook the glass at me for more.

I took her out to the dining area, carrying the wine by the neck like a dinner bell, and pulled out a chair for her. "Madame!" I went. I placed the bottle on the table.

"Oui, oui!" she went. Papa Wally must have taught the gals some pidgin French.

I went back to the kitchen, turned off the stove and heaped stew and carrots on a pair of plates. When I returned, she was chug-a-lugging right out of the bottle and let loose with a hearty belch after finishing.

She reached into the stew and grabbed a potato with her fingers, and then dropped it, and licked her fingers. "Hot!"

"Let me get you a spoon."

I found silverware in the kitchen, but by the time I came back out, she had already eaten about half of the stew with her fingers, her head near the plate. She picked up the now-empty bottle and waved it at me.

"Go slow," I said. "That wine will creep up on you."

"You say that like it's bad," she said, and looked up from the plate, her chin dripping, smiling wolfishly.

I handed her a spoon, and she watched me, the way I held it and ate, and imitated me. She wiped her chin with a cloth napkin that had been left on the table. She licked the spoon like a lollypop when she was done, and then licked down the plate. "More wine!" she demanded, and pounded the table with her fist.

"You may have a little French in you," I said.

"Take that back," she snapped. "Take it back now."

"I take it back," I said quickly.

"Those monkeys. What they did to them," she said, getting serious. "That was really bad!"

"I'll get more wine," I said.

"Russo! Americans aren't like that, are they?"

"I didn't use to think we were. But we've done some terrible things. They felt necessary. But they were terrible."

"Have *you* done terrible things?"

I looked down at the deck, searching through my mind for an answer that wasn't "Yes." I couldn't find it. I could feel her staring at me. My face stung. "Yes."

"Okay," she said a beat later, her voice wobbling a bit with drink and rage. "Go get more wine."

I looked over at her, but she wasn't looking at me. She was looking at her licked-clean plate and empty wine glass.

I went into the storage room and heard glass smashing. I ran out with a new bottle in my hand. She'd thrown the empty against the bulkhead. I set the bottle down and ran over to her, and stopped short. She stumbled up out of her chair, the legs screeching against the teak deck, and put her arms around me. "I don't want you to be a bad man," she said.

"Then I won't." I held her lightly.

"I want you to be good."

"I'll be good. I swear."

She reached behind herself and unzipped the dress and let it fall to the floor. "I don't want to wear that anymore. I want my grass skirt back." She stepped out of the dress and kicked it drunkenly away. She picked up a cloth dinner napkin and wiped the makeup off her face. She cried a bit and blew her nose in the napkin and tossed that across the room, too. "Those poor monkeys. That poor man in the radio room!"

"I'm sorry, sweetheart." I tried to kiss her, but she gently pushed me away. She sat down in the chair, laid her head in her arms next to the empty dinner plate which had slid gradually to port, belched lightly and fell asleep.

The Nazi Escapes!

I decided that I didn't want her sleeping there, so I picked her up and carried her up one more flight, back to the passenger cabins. I found a room with a double bed and tucked her in, pulling the sheets up to her chin. I stroked her face with the tips of my fingers, until she fluttered her hand at me. I left her to rest.

I went through the rooms again, found a backpack, and dumped out the contents. I filled it up with cigarettes, a flask of some sort of fragrant green liquor, underwear and socks. Tossed the Kraut popgun in there, too, along with the gauze and tape. I found the officers' quarters. The captain was a strapping man like me, so I found a new set of khakis and a new pair of boondocker boots, a half-size too tight. I figured they'd stretch out. I put on my new uniform and felt better. I found a safety razor, a brush and some shaving soap. A little drizzle of water came out of the tap. I plugged the sink and I used the water to shave. I slapped on some bay rum, too. In the mirror, my bruise was already turning from purple to yellow.

I went back to the room with the Kraut in it and found Judy and Toshiro snuggled up in a corner, snoozing peacefully. I chased away a soldier who was standing over Judy, masturbating while staring at her nude body. What I didn't find was the Kraut. He was gone.

I shook the little couple awake. "Hey, Ike! Mamie! Rise

and shine."

"Wha-?" Judy went.

"Some turnkey you turned out to be," I said. "Where's the Nazi?"

She rubbed her eyes and looked for a moment like a kitten left mewing in a picnic basket on a neighbor's doorstep. "I was tired."

"Apparently, our German friend wasn't. He hightailed it out of here."

"No," Toshiro said, sitting up. He quickly rose to his feet and retrieved his rifle.

"Go find him!"

He looked down at Judy, as if for permission.

"Go!" I shouted at him. "Find the Kraut!"

He sprinted out the door onto the deck of the ship and stopped. "Here!"

"That was quick," I said to Judy. "Impressive, your new boyfriend." She rolled her eyes and snorted.

I reached over, pinched her cheek and she slapped my hand away. "Cut it out!"

I dug the Luger out of the backpack and walked out on

the deck. I needn't have bothered to arm myself. He was standing there with a pair of binoculars, looking out to sea. "I dare say that you're psychic, Herr Russo." He'd taken off his jacket and hat and rolled up his sleeves. He pointed, and handed me the binoculars. I shoved the pistol in my belt.

I looked through the glasses and saw a submarine's sail adorned with a red star. "Commies!"

Typical Commies!

"They have been sitting there like that for hours," von Schlechteren said. "Perhaps, I think, they are reticent to come to shore without orders."

"Typical commies. Probably have to radio back to Moscow to get permission to take a dump."

I waved over Toshiro. He set his rifle down on the deck. I handed him the binoculars and pointed out the Russian sub.

"You smell like bay rum and Mutterleib," the Kraut noted. "I like your new clothes, however." He sniffed a bit more. "And you smell like Goulash! And wine!"

"Go down to the galley. There's plenty there. I wouldn't recommend going down to the hold. Those Frogs are dangerous. You run into any of their monkeys?"

"Yes, I have. Their work is based on Nazi science. We had a lab in Borneo. The helmets were meant for human use."

"You had a hand in that?"

"I'm not a scientist. I'm an... administrator. And a poor one at that. It's how I ended up here. It was easier than sending me back to Berlin to be shot. I was a schoolteacher before the Nazis. Frankly, I'm a coward. It was easier to go along. If you made the right noises in Germany, they would give you a fancy uniform."

"You have an Iron Cross."

"That is a long story, mein freund. I shall tell you some day of what I did to receive that decoration."

"After you eat, you should find some civvies, get that uniform off." I gave him a serious look. "Heena's in bed down there. Leave her alone."

"That is not a problem, Herr Russo. You see, my kind also ended up in the concentration camps."

"You're clearly not a gypsy."

"Let us say that my proclivities would have put me there."

It finally dawned on me what he meant. "Oh."

"Yes," he said. "'Oh,' indeed."

Hiro and the rest of the soldiers lined up on deck. Hiro stood at the front of the small formation and called them to attention. He performed an about face and saluted me. I took his salute. I gave him a quick brief on the Soviet sub and what their intentions were. He turned back to his men, briefed them, and by the sound of it, set a watch schedule.

When his men had fallen out, and one of them relieved Toshiro of the binoculars, Hiro turned to me and asked, "Where is Ruby?"

I put a hand on his shoulder. "She's with Dottie and Sandy. I imagine she's already back in the village and getting ready to hit the hay by now."

"Ruby, baby," he said. "She is hot stuff."

"I think you two could have some good looking kids."

That perked him up some. "Little ones," he said, smiling contentedly.

"We've got to get through this first, though."

That brought him back to his military bearing. He clicked his heels and bowed. I looked around at the men who were still on the deck. The sense of purpose that had been lacking in their lives was now being filled. They looked like men again. "We are hungry, Russo-san."

"There's chow down in the galley," I said. "Wait a minute though." I walked over to the masturbator and grabbed him by the collar. "No more of that shit," I said, wagging a finger in his face. "You know what I'm saying."

Hiro translated. He cast his eyes down. He spoke a few words of Japanese. Hiro said, "He swears on his honor that he will not do what you caught him doing again by the ladies."

I let go of his collar, smoothed out his uniform some. "You're good men. I can tell. Let's all perform our duty when the time comes." Hiro translated that, and the men all nodded at me appreciatively.

I decided to go crawl into bed with Heena. I was asleep on my feet, plus I wanted to put that particular temptation out of reach for the horny soldiers.

Judy, for her part, had put on the Kraut's Nazi jacket and it went down past her knees. Her tiny arms disappeared in the sleeves. A cool breeze blew in off the Pacific as the sun went down. Toshiro stood with her. "Get a room, you two," I said. "Go down the aft ladder. Plenty of rooms down there. You should find something to wear other than that Nazi coat."

Judy shrugged. "It's warm."

I took Toshiro aside. "Be gentle with her, big guy."

"Bronco Nagurski," he agreed, shaking his head yes. "Wayne Millner."

"And flowers. Don't forget the flowers."

"Andy Pilney!" he said to that.

Battle Plan for the Soviet Invasion of Paradise!

I went down to the cabin. Heena was in the head, shitting her brains out, door closed. The French food apparently didn't settle properly in her guts. I hoped there'd be enough water in the tank for the toilet to flush, or it would be an unpleasant evening. "Pull the chain!" I called in to her.

I sat down on a wing chair, blue with gold fleur-de-lis accents, took off my new, tight boots, and propped my feet up on the bed.

The toilet flushed and Heena emerged. "That canned French slop gave me the trots, Russo," she said. "Woo-ee!"

"Yeah, I heard you in there. Feel better?"

She walked over and curled up in my lap, her head on my shoulder, her brown arms around my neck. I held her like that for a while, running my fingertips up and down her sleek body. She kissed me and got up. "Come to bed," she said.

"In a minute. I've got some thinking to do."

"Suit yourself." She crawled to the far side of the bed, her lovely derriere wiggling, squirmed between the sheets, lay on her side facing me, an arm languidly stretched across my side of the bed, and closed her sparkling eyes. She still seemed a little drunk. In a moment, I heard her snoring charmingly.

I lit a cigarette from one of the packs I'd pilfered and sat smoking for a while, thinking about the Soviets just off shore, and my responsibilities to my new troops. We'd have to consolidate our forces back at the village, maybe dig in. We'd have to figure out how to defend the place with one round of ammo, which was apparently chambered in the Luger in my backpack. And the Nazi. I wasn't sure what to think of him. He'd seemed pretty convincing when he'd threatened me, and more convincing when he wasn't threatening me. As long as he wasn't wearing that disgusting uniform, I suppose I'd be okay with him for the time being. When our guys came ashore, I'd definitely turn him over. I didn't fight in that theater of the war, but by this time in human history we all knew what the SS had done, and he must have done something pretty atrocious to get that Iron Cross.

I got up and paced around some in my stocking feet, smoking a second cigarette while I did so, all these thoughts whirling through my noggin.

On an impulse, I slid open the top drawer of the dresser and found a number of fashionable scarves in there. I pulled one out that had a pink and turquoise pattern on it. I shook it out, and discovered it would be more than sufficient to wrap around Heena's waist. If she wasn't going to wear a dress, I could at least have her wear this thing. I placed it on the bed, along with a couple more scarves for her to choose from, took off my shirt and pants and got into bed with her. She unconsciously slipped an arm across my torso and draped a leg across one of mine, said, "Russo," with a little groan, and we slept like that until the shipboard alarm went off a few hours later, a voice on the 1MC shouting, "The Russians! The Russians!"

The Nazi Plan to Dissect Island Girls!

I went topside and found the German there, binoculars out, looking serenely unconcerned. I tied my boots and buttoned my shirt.

"So?"

"False alarm," the Kraut said. He was dressed like the Frenchmen now—white linen suit, black tie, black oxfords. He'd shaved as well. He looked sleek and elegant in his newfound clothes, like he might start discussing the merits of Wittgenstein over a Chablis.

Heena appeared at my side. She'd tied the scarf I'd liked around her waist and found, somewhere, a scarlet flower to slip into her hair. "Where are the Russians?" she asked.

"Still on their sub," I said. Or maybe they slipped

ashore under cover of darkness. I didn't say that aloud. "Are you feeling better this morning?" I placed a palm on her forehead. Her head was cool and dry. We smooched quickly.

"Yah, real good," she said. "We're letting the glass eye man roam free?" She threw him a suspicious glare, with a hint of warning in it.

"For now. Let me see your foot." She'd taken the gauze off of it. She balanced on one foot and proffered her wounded foot. There was no wound, not even a sign of one. I could see where the tape had been, so it wasn't the wrong foot. I checked her wrists and there was no sign that she'd ever had ropes binding her. "This is incredible."

"Ah, her healing powers," the German said. "Part of the reason I was sent here was that the Japanese reported to us that there were girl children here who did not wound easily and could heal quickly. This was of interest to the high command."

I bent down and squinted at her foot. She placed a hand on my head to keep herself balanced. I licked my finger and rubbed at the spot. There was no scaring either. "I can't believe it."

"My orders were to have the girls dissected," he said.

I quickly looked up at him and let go of Heena's foot. I stood up. For a moment there, I wanted to kill him with my bare hands.

"Obviously I didn't," he said, taking a step back. "Instead, I hid out in the jungle. I've been hiding all this time. I'm not a good Nazi, I suppose. I thought that if I could present them with the atomic dingus, perhaps I could go home..." His voice trailed off.

"Dissect us?" Heena asked. "You mean cut us up? Put us in jars?"

"There were a lot of orders that I simply ignored," he said, not looking at either of us.

"Civilization!" Heena exclaimed with disgust. "You can have it!"

Apes Grab Judy!

Heena and I held hands like teenagers.

The Japanese soldiers stood on the deck in a tight little formation with Hiro at the lead. He barked out orders to them. Toshiro was AWOL. So was little Judy. I heard some shouting coming from over the side and looked down. Toshiro was down there in an outrigger canoe, paddling furiously, hollering in Japanese.

"What is it?" I asked Hiro.

"He is saying, 'Help me!'"

"Where's Judy?" Heena asked.

Hiro shouted down to Toshiro. Toshiro replied.

"He says the monkeys took her," Hiro said.

"Did any of your men find guns or ammo on this tub?" I asked Hiro.

"No, Russo-san," he said.

"What about cans of that knockout gas?"

"Knockout gas?" I did my best to describe the cans to them. "No, Russo-san. No knockout gas."

"I'm going to go get Judy. Who's on my team?"

"I am," Heena said. The way she looked, there would be no argument. I wanted to keep her close anyway.

"Who else?"

Toshiro raised his hand, and Hiro.

"Otto, I guess that leaves you in charge here. Keep an

eye on the Russians. If they come ashore, set a fire near the beach with old palm fronds to signal us and then scoot on out of here. We'll rally at the village and figure out how to keep them away from that dingus. It'll be bad news for our side if the Reds get their hands on that thing."

"Ja wohl, Herr Russo."

"It's Russ, big guy. Thanks for not carving up my lady."

"Of course, er... Russ. We'll see you at the village."

Heena Takes Charge!

After loading up my backpack and the soldiers' with provisions, we climbed down the rope into the outrigger canoe. Heena came down last, automatically grabbed the oar and started rowing. She did it so quickly and expertly that none of us menfolk had time to object to allowing a lady to do our work. "Where'd this boat come from anyway?" I asked Hiro.

"I can answer that, Russo," Heena said, while paddling the canoe forward effortlessly. She wasn't even breaking a sweat and it seemed like we were going about ten knots toward shore. "I made it." She stopped rowing for a second and thumped the interior of the canoe with a knuckle. Her name was burnt in neat script.

Hiro shrugged sheepishly. "It is a nice boat, Heena."

"You shoulda asked me for it instead of stealing it, Hiro. Woulda given it to ya."

"Sorry."

"That's all right. We had some laughs."

I felt a prickle of jealousy, and then let it go.

We came ashore and all leapt out of the boat and dragged it onto the beach. "I thought all the old ones died before they could show you how to build these things," I said.

"They did," Heena said. "I read how to do it in the *Encyclopedia Britannica*. Nice set of books." She walked over to Hiro, snatched his rifle out of his hands and popped off the bayonet. "I'm gonna need this for a second or two. Unlike *some people* I can name, I return stuff." She walked over to a stand of bamboo and skillfully whacked one down in a couple of strokes. She whittled one end of the bamboo to a point, and then handed the new spear to me. "Know how to handle this thing?"

"Probably not," I said, hefting it in my mitts.

"You have a lot to learn. But since you're such nice eye candy, I think I'll keep you around." She grasped me under my chin with her free hand, puckered my lips for me, and gave me a quick kiss, followed by a solicitous pat on the cheek. She quickly cut herself a bamboo spear, flipped the bayonet over and handed it back to Hiro grip first. He mounted it onto his rusty rifle.

I walked over to the pile of clothes we'd left behind the previous day and noticed that Judy's grass skirt was missing. At least she was clothed, I thought. I found my Brooklyn Dodgers hat and put that on. I dug out my lighter and wallet.

"Dodgers!" Toshiro said. "Babe Herman!"

"I'm a White Sox fan, born and bred," I said.

"Black Sox. Cheaters!" Toshiro said. "Shoeless Joe!"

"You want a sock in the kisser, mac? Take that back!"

"Sorry, Russo-san."

"If you two are finished, I'd like to go save my sister. If that's okay with you."

"Yes, dear," I said.

"Try to keep up," she said, and leapt off into the brush like a gazelle, crying out, "Yi-yi-yi-yi-yi!"

Tiny Woman Staked Out by Apes!

We found Judy staked out in a jungle clearing, her tiny hands and feet each roped to a large tent peg. Heena took a knee and quickly untied Judy's arms while Toshiro untied her legs.

"You broke your promise," Judy said, looking at me crossly. "You promised you wouldn't let me get kidnapped again, yet here I am, tied up by a buncha monkeys! They weren't very nice about it either."

"Where are they?" I asked, right before three cans of billowing smoke dropped around us, and the world turned dim and gray.

Carved-Up Brains Create Ape Mates!

I awoke back at the French camp. Doctor Maurice Thuilière stood sweating before me as I blinked the sleep out of my eyes. His wattles trembled under his chin, his face glistening with rivulets of fear sweat. "I do apologize, mon ami, for the mistreatment you have suffered at the hands of my creations."

"I'm not your pal, Doctor. And you're out of your goddamned mind."

"You could say the same for my friends Jean and Yves," he said with an ironic chuckle. I looked past the doctor and saw Jean in the dirt, clearly dead, blood and brain matter surrounding him. Yves was standing bolt upright, staring blankly into the jungle, or at least in that general direction. He had one of the helmets drilled into his head. His face was bloodlessly pale, like a sheet of typing paper. One of the monkeys stood beside him with the control device, twisting the dial. As he did so, Yves took a step forward and then took a step back.

An operating table just like the one aboard the ship was near the monkey and the two men. Bloody tools were on a card table nearby.

"What the hell is going on here, doctor? Where's my wife? Where's Toshiro and Hiro?"

"Well, your wife... the apes they want her for themselves. The little one? She was only the bait. Too small! You see, the apes are quite choosy in their choice of mates. César there? He wants only the Dottie. He craves her and now he sends the little one back to the village for her and only her. You see? It is so simple! The apes desire, and will soon have these women for themselves. I am now just a pawn in their operation."

"How the hell did you let this happen?"

"I perhaps enjoy the wine too much? And soon they overwhelm me and my friends. César, he make me operate on both my friends to see them suffer, perhaps, and perhaps to see if the operation work on human beings. As you can see, it does."

"Where's Heena?" I was tied tightly to a tree.

"She will soon be on the operating table. You see we have it outside in the fresh air, and not in the tent, where she is tied up at the moment."

"Where's Toshiro and Hiro?"

"The apes, they want to use them for, how you say? Target practice. Yes, the apes have discovered love and therefore impétuosité. They will throw the bamboo spears at them until they are dead, I'm afraid. Who could have predicted such an outcome? I give these apes the great gift of the French language, all of its beauty and le charme, and now they turn upon me in a most scandaleux fashion!"

The monkeys grew quiet suddenly, and the doctor turned and looked. César, the biggest of them all, stood in the middle of his clan as they gathered around. They all peered off into the jungle. César picked up a fez and affixed it on his head. He twisted the dial and Yves took off his jacket, vest, tie and shirt. He dressed up César in his clothes, becoming a valet to the monkey, tying a half Windsor around his neck. The ape decided to go without pants and shoes.

A procession of apes arrived, singing:

Nous sommes des dégourdis,

Nous sommes des lascars

Des types pas ordinaires.

Nous avons souvent notre cafard,

Nous sommes les singes.

Upon their shoulders, they carried Dottie, clearly unconscious from more knockout gas. I struggled with my ropes, but the apes were better at knots that most of the humans I'd met on the island, so my ropes only became tighter. "Dottie!" I shouted at her. "Wake up! Wake up!" I knew she could take the apes in a fair fight, but there was nothing fair about any of this.

An ape appeared beside me and gave me a solicitous pat with his paw. On his shoulder, he carried the limp Judy, sweetly snoozing. He set her down carefully beside me, resting her head on my shoulder. "Ne bougez pas," he said. He reached out and playfully pinched her nose, and then went to join his fellow apes around Dottie, who they were now strapping to the operating table with nylon belts. The table pivoted and until it appeared Dottie was standing. An ape brought out a bowl, soap and a straight razor.

"How much of that knockout gas did you guys bring?" I asked the doctor.

"You did not ask what the apes were planning for you, mon ami."

"I don't care."

"They plan on eating your brain and your liver. They

believe they can take from you la robustesse."

"Swell. But if I get out of these ropes, I swear I'll take all of their lives, and yours, too, you French fink!"

"I believe I am needed in surgery. I bid you, adieu!"

I jostled Judy with my shoulder, trying to wake her up. "Judy!" I whisper-hissed at her. "Wake up! Untie me!"

I looked up in time to see them shaving the sides of Dottie's head. Her head was held in place by leather straps across her chin and forehead. "Prenez vos pattes outre ses singes vous sacrément sale!" I shouted at them, to no avail.

César stepped up on a rock and proclaimed, "Je suis l'orateur de la loi!"

The apes stopped what they were doing, and gave him a round of applause. "Vive l'orateur! Plus! Plus!"

"Quelle est la loi?" César asked, his hands extended, his head tilted.

"Pour prendre les femmes pour nous-mêmes!" the ape with the straight razor answered.

"Oui! Telle est la loi!" César shouted, to cheers and great applause from the apes.

I struggled more with the ropes and they became tighter and tighter. Judy's head fell into my lap. "Toshiro!

My binky-boo!" she called out in her sleep.

Dottie's eyelids fluttered and she came out of her slumber in time to see le docteur Maurice Thuilière pick up a hand-cranked drill. "My apologies," he said, without a hint of apology in his voice. "It is my duty to inform you that you will be married, soon, to this fine ape."

César doffed his fez and bowed deeply.

"The hell I will!" Dottie roared.

"You will have no choice in the matter, mon cher, as la volonté will no longer be yours." He placed the business end of the drill against her temple, and just as he was about to start cranking, his hand exploded.

I snapped my head quickly to my right and saw, standing in the clearing, a short man wearing khaki shorts, sneakers with no socks, a dark blue shirt with the word NAVY in gold letters across the chest, and a khaki baseball cap tucked smartly on his head. He wore a pair of dark Ray Bans. A pistol belt around his waist held a holster, ammo pouches and a knife in a scabbard. The baseball cap sported a pair of silver railroad tracks. In his hand was a Colt M1911 semi-automatic, with smoke wisping out of the barrel. A filterless cigarette dangled languidly from the corner of his mouth, also wisping smoke.

Pepper of the Navy!

The doctor fell to the ground, holding his wrist, howling in agony.

The apes shrieked loudly, leaping and bounding about the campsite in an inchoate rage.

César, the lead ape, retrieved the dial from his pocket, but before he could do anything with it, the Navyman shot the device out of his hand, and now both the ape and his former master were missing appendages, and watching blood spurt from their wrists. Lt. Buzz Pepper whipped off the Ray Bans, revealing his girlish eyes.

"Buzz!" I shouted over at him. "Watch yourself! These apes speak French!"

"I know!" he said, letting the dangling cigarette drop to the loamy soil. "I had a couple of lovely gals bring over something to rectify that situation."

Ruby and Sandy appeared out of the jungle toting the atomic dingus. They set it down horizontally next to Buzz, who pulled a key out of his pocket and unlocked the bottom. The apes organized themselves into a little brigade, and were just beginning to charge when Buzz pushed a button and a loud metallic squeal blasted out of the dingus.

The apes all grabbed their heads and, with blood shooting from their nostrils and ears, collapsed in a heap, all of them dead.

The doctor, miraculously still alive, rose to his feet clutching his wrist and sprinted off in the opposite direction. Buzz raised his weapon, but Sandy pushed it back down. "Let him go," Sandy said. "I know exactly where he's heading, and he ain't gonna get far."

Buzz holstered his weapon, sprinted over to Dottie, and cut her loose with his knife.

"You're a sight for sore eyes, lieutenant," she said, and then took him into her arms, dipped him and kissed him passionately for what seemed like a minute or two.

She brought him back up and let him go. He staggered in place for a moment, gasping for breath, and then said, "Brother, the natives sure are friendly on this island!" He picked up the knife where he'd dropped it on the ground.

"I'm tied up over here, but take your time… *lieutenant*," I said.

Judy woke up, sat up and peered around through sleep-dimmed eyes. "Did I miss everything?" She rubbed her eyes adorably and yawned, also adorably. I had an overwhelming urge to pinch the dickens out of her dimpled cheeks, but I was still bound to the tree.

"Heena!" I called out. "Heena!"

"I'm in here, Russo!" Her voice came from the tent.

Judy untied me. I thanked her quickly, gave her a pinch on the cheek, which she slapped away, and sprinted to the tent, where I found Heena on a cot, tied up. I picked up a penknife and cut her loose and we were quickly in each other's arms. "What happened out there?"

"That dingus? It killed the monkeys!"

"How come we're still alive?"

"I can answer that," Lt. Buzz Pepper said, standing by the tent flap.

We heard, off in the distance, the Frenchman's voice calling out, "Aidez moi! Help!" We followed Sandy down an unfamiliar trail and found the Frenchman neck deep in quicksand, his one good hand reaching out toward us.

"Should we save him?" Heena asked.

"No," Sandy said. "He's bad. Very bad!"

Dottie pushed us all out of the way and threw him the

end of a rope. There seemed to be no shortage of rope on this island. His hand gripped it momentarily, and then down he went, into the muck. A bubble burped up out of the quicksand and the Frenchman was gone.

Twice a Traitor!

We stood staring at the quicksand, not quite believing what we'd seen. There was a lot to take in, actually, with the dead monkeys and all. Sandy broke the silence.

"I love your skirt!" she told Heena.

"It's the latest fashion for 1955!" Heena said, doing a spin for her, biting her bottom lip and fluttering her considerable eyelashes.

We walked back to the campsite down the trail, the sides of which were littered with the contorted bodies of apes, their helmets blown out, some still smoking. Heena and I held hands as we walked along. She trembled a bit, and I wrapped my arm around her shoulders. "Don't look," I told her.

"Okay," she said.

"You don't want to remember this."

"That's for sure."

"You're twice a traitor," I said to Pepper.

"You sting me, brother! How am *I* a traitor?" Pepper seemed unfazed by all the dead apes and destruction. Just another day at the office for a Navy lieutenant, I guess. He flipped a Lucky Strike into his mouth, produced a kitchen match from his pocket and struck it on a palm tree as we strode by.

"First, you join the Navy. The Navy! And second, you go and become an officer!"

"I could point out that you're an officer in the merchant marine," Pepper said. He took a long drag off the Lucky and let it out, saying, "But that's enough hen party gabbing, we got work to do." He flicked the half-smoked cigarette onto a dead monkey's back.

"Oh, yah! And how!" Dottie said, placing her hands on Pepper's shoulders from behind. "You gotta take me back to the village and wash my feet."

"I'm sure there's a significance to this I'm not catching," Pepper said. "But, hell, it's jake with me. I'll wash your feet for you, baby! Anytime, anywhere!"

"That's the spirit, little man," Dottie said, leaning down and giving him a peck on the cheek. "I like your pluck."

"And I like your... everything. My God, the size of you! It's like God packed two women into one and the result is four times better than any woman alive! I have to warn you, I play for keeps and I play for now. I came from nowhere and that's where I'm heading."

"You silver-tongued imp!"

Heena gave my chest a squeeze and I glanced down at her. She was smiling beatifically. She was happy for her big sister, I think.

"I have about a million questions for you before you start canoodling," I said. "Starting with that atomic dingus and how it killed those monkeys."

"That dingus is the XAD-53, produced under the auspices of the Atomic Energy Commission. Imagine a device that can knock every fighter out of the sky within ten miles. Not only that, but every electronic device in that radius... ten miles up and ten miles across! We intended to test it out at an atoll about 500 miles thataway, but some loose lips sunk our ship, and the Russkies tried to get their greasy mitts on it." Buzz smirked. "Not in my Navy! Not only did I kill all those monkeys, but I shorted out that Red sub on the other side of the island."

"How'd you know about that sub?"

"Saw it when I swam ashore. Ran across some dimwitted squares who, when I threatened to sock them all in the kisser, told me exactly where to find the XAD-53. So I tracked down Dottie, Sandy and Ruby. Friendly chicks! Mighty friendly chicks! Dottie immediately shouts, 'I call him!' and Sandy gets all pouty. But what the hey. Look at Dottie!" he said, turning to his girl, who stood a head taller than him. "My God!"

She skipped up alongside him, took off his ballcap and put it on her own head. She winked at Buzz, ruffled his hair like he was her little brother.

"I'm weak in the knees!" Buzz said. "Weak!"

"So the Navy sent just you?" I said.

"I've had special training. With all your talk about the romance of the sea when we were bunkies in the hospital, and no work for an illustrator back home, I thought I'd give the Navy a whirl. The recruiter asked me if I had any special talents, so I told him about being able to draw and how, as a kid, I could juggle and walk a tightrope. Common enough skills back home in Sarasota, where we have the circus during the winter months. They asked me if I'd like to be on a special team and become a frogman. I said, 'Sure! I got nothing to do for the next couple of decades. My calendar is clear.' So they sign me up for this 'UDT Six.' Now I do this sort of mission all the time." He leaned over to me and asked confidentially, "By the way, you haven't seen a Professor Greenwood around these parts, have you? Snooty Britisher in a lab coat? I'm always running across that bird."

"No," I said. "But I bet he's around the next corner, if my current lucky streak is holding true."

We came back into the campsite and found Ruby and Hiro, and Toshiro and Judy, all having a fine time getting reacquainted among the monkey ruins. The shock had killed Yves as well. He lay amongst the dead monkeys, who were all in a heap.

"Look!" Hiro shouted, pointing.

Human Sacrifice!

A thin tendril of smoke rose from the location of the French ship. "Russians coming!" Toshiro said.

"Guess they couldn't wait any longer to hear from Moscow once they lost electrics on that tub," Pepper said. "Time for you gals and the Japanese soldiers to head back to the village, gather our forces."

"What about the dingus?" I asked.

Pepper walked over to it, popped it open. All the electrics in it were fried. "The girls should take it with them anyway," he said. "The Reds might be able to reverse engineer it, like they did the A-bomb. Meanwhile, daddy-o, you and me will stage a surprise along the trail for the Russians."

At that moment, the ground shook violently. The gals all turned and genuflected toward the volcano. "Mondo Tiki, Tiki Mondo!" they chanted.

"Mondo speaks!" Dottie said.

"What does he say?" Heena asked.

In answer, a red jet of flame burst from the top of the volcano and a massive spurt of molten rock was flung into the air. It arced in the direction of the smoke, French ship and submarine, screaming like an artillery shell, and landed a few moments later with a loud report, shaking the earth enough to toss us violently off our feet. We picked ourselves up.

The ground stopped shaking and the smoke from

Mondo Tiki slowed to its usual steady billow of steam, like a massive simmering tea kettle.

"Holy mackerel!" Buzz exclaimed.

"You gals aren't thinking about sacrificing one of you to Mondo Tiki, are you?" I asked.

"You mean like jumping into Mondo's tummy?" Judy asked.

"Oh good golly, no!" Heena said.

"What makes you say that, beefcake?" Dottie asked.

"I don't know. Movies?"

"Movies!" Heena said, shaking her head. "The things that come out of your mouth!" Now it was *my* turn to get my cheek pinched. "Good thing you're so handsome! Might have to throw you back into the sea where I found you."

The Magnificent Four!

"It's about time for you gals and your Japanese chums to put an egg in your shoe and beat it," Buzz said. "Me and Private Russo need to take on the Soviet army."

"Not without *our* help," Dottie said.

"Darlin', it's important to get that weapon stashed! That's the big mission, and I'm counting on you gals to get it done. We've got more frogmen coming this way. Heck, we've got a task force heading this way," he said, looking at his watch. He tapped on the watch a couple of times and then took it off and chucked it onto the pile of dead monkeys. "Keeps on ticking, my puckered ass," he muttered. "Anyway, we need that device gone and we need you gals to stay safe. Peace of mind and all!"

"What about our peace of mind?" Sandy asked. "Maybe some of us don't want to see you menfolk get killed over some dingus. Maybe some of us think you're the cutest little lieutenant ever, with the prettiest eyes of any boy we've ever seen."

"Hey! Hands off!" Dottie said. "I called him fair and square!"

"Yeah, yeah! Jeez-oh-man, when is it Sandy's turn? I ask you!" She looked around at all the happy couples and made a sad face. Heena walked over and put her arms around her, and then so did Judy, Ruby and finally Dottie.

"Didn't you hear what I was saying?" Buzz asked. "The

Navy's coming! You want all-American men? Dig it, dolls, they're heading this way and how!"

They fell out of each other's embrace. Dottie and Sandy picked up the XAD-53 with the makeshift stretcher. The gals lined up.

Hiro walked over to us. "I stay!"

Ruby shouted, "No!" She sprinted over and grabbed his hand, tried to pull him away from us. She let go and backed away, her hands over her mouth.

Toshiro quickly followed him over. "I stay, too!"

"No, you cats need to keep the gals safe," Buzz said.

"We stay! We're soldiers! We fight!" Hiro said.

Buzz slapped each man on the shoulder. "By God, I'm glad you're on our side now. Rusty rifles, but you choose to stay." He shook each of their hands—a good handshake by the look of it. Solid. Ruby and Judy looked stricken.

"Ruby, baby!" Hiro said. "I make you proud!"

"Judy, pretty Judy!" Toshiro said. He ran over and embraced her. "Jim Thorpe!" he said, stepping back, thumping his chest. "Jesse Owens!"

"I swear I have no idea what he's talking about," Judy said, a tear trickling down her cheek.

Heena walked over and kissed me softly, but passionately. "You stay alive, Russo."

Dottie set down the dingus and ran over to Buzz, wrapped her arms around him and lifted him up off the ground. They kissed. She set him down, spun him around and slapped him on the behind. "Go get'm, tiger!" She and Sandy picked up the device and they and their sisters trotted off into the jungle, leaving us four former enemies together to fight our new common enemy. I watched until I couldn't see Heena anymore. I felt the air go out of me.

"So do you soldiers have any rounds for those rifles?" Buzz asked.

"No brass, no ammo," Toshiro said.

"We hunted," Hiro said. "We ate fruit. We waited. No one came. No more orders."

"We're here now, shipmates," Buzz said. "Let's survive this and get you men a trip back home. Let's all remember what we're fighting for."

"GIRLS!" Toshiro shouted.

Then we all raised our fists and shouted as one, "GIRLS!"

Mondo Scores a Direct Hit!

We went through the tent, and the various wooden boxes surrounding it, looking for guns, ammo... guns and ammo. I found some 9-mm ammunition, so I loaded the well-oiled Luger's magazine and snapped it into place. In a box, we found a pair of bolt-action Mauser rifles in perfect shape, gooped in purple cosmoline, along with boxes of ammo. I guess the Frenchmen didn't have that much faith in Nazi science, but were too lazy to get the firearms into working order. I gave the rifles to Hiro and Toshiro, who immediately went about cleaning them with the kits stowed in the bottom of the box.

I watched Buzz jog up a coconut tree in much the same fashion as Heena. He'd acquired a pair of binoculars from the French and peered in the direction of the ship and sub. "I'll be goddamned," he said. "I think ol' Mondo Tiki is on our side."

"Why do you say that?"

"Mondo scored a direct hit on the commie sub! It's on fire!"

"That may be the Oberleutnant doing his own personal march on Moscow."

"Oberleutnant? Is there a Nazi on this island, too?"

"Damn skippy."

"Is he on the French freighter?"

"Yeah."

"That's on fire, too."

"I hope he got off of there." We heard the pop and crack of small arms fire off in the distance. "Maybe we need the gals to call in another strike by the volcano god."

"Wouldn't hurt." Buzz dropped his partially spent magazine, caught it expertly, and loaded a full magazine from his belt with a satisfying snap forward of the bolt, all while balancing on the bent tree.

"We show you place," Toshiro said.

"We have many bunkers, dug many years ago to defend the island," Hiro said.

We gathered up our supplies, including cans of French food, water and our weaponry. We walked out on the main trail, the one that went from Mondo Tiki village to the French encampment, and on down to Maui Tiki beach.

Buzz popped a stick of Black Jack into his mouth, and

then offered me one.

"You got extra pockets in those shorts I don't know about?" I asked him.

"You been studying my shorts, shipmate?"

"Maybe a little."

"Maybe Dottie busts you in the chops for looking."

"Let's keep it our little secret then." I lit one of my French cigarettes and puffed on it for a while. We marched along for about a quarter mile before coming to a slight dip in the trail, followed by a slight rise.

At the middle of the rise, Hiro and Toshiro hopped off the trail. Hiro reached into the dirt, moss and leaves and lifted up a handle, and there was a pre-dug position. A similar one was on the other side of the trail.

"High ground," Buzz said. "I like it."

"Every 15 meters," Hiro said, gesturing up the trail. We talked tactics for a while, deciding that we would cover Hiro and Toshiro while they beat feet, and then they would do the same for us.

Buzz and I slipped into one trench, and Hiro and Toshiro slipped into the other. "Don't shoot until you see the whites of their eyes."

"Field of fire," Toshiro said, gesturing.

The Truth About Papa Wally!

We each closed our lids and could look out through a slit. It was dark in there, and smelled like someone took a dump in it recently. I wondered if the girls knew about these. Maybe one of these is where they hid the dingus originally.

"You haven't been to the village yet, have you?"

"No," Buzz said. "I did get an earful about how smart 'Papa Wally' is."

"He's a tubby little rum-runner from Wisconsin," I said. "Worked for Capone way back when."

"Wait a minute. Are we talking about Waldo Bostick? *The* Waldo Bostick?"

"Yeah. You've heard of him?"

"Didn't you go to the movies when you were a kid?

Watch the newsreels?"

"Not really. Mostly worked in my pop's butcher shop on weekends. Why?"

"Hell, and you from Chicago and all! Seriously, his name doesn't ring a bell at all with you?"

"It kind of did when he first told me. My pop avoided the rackets. He made an honest living. Thought the gangsters gave us Italians a bad name."

"This is like a bad gag! Wally Bostick was an inventor of sorts. He invented the pyramid scheme! Combined with the numbers racket, he made a killing back in the 1920's, and double-crossed Capone himself. It's said he got away with a cool million and disappeared. Now we know where he disappeared to, don't we?"

"You don't think he's got the loot buried here, do you?"

"I don't know what to think. But if it's cash money, it may have gone to jungle rot in this little paradise."

"I have a feeling he sank it in the sea. Maybe put it where the pearl beds are located, wherever that is."

"Why's that?"

"A story the girls told, more like a tall tale, about how

the island was created. And he told me that the original natives, the ones he pretty much killed off with a case of the flu, thought it was taboo to go pearl diving. I don't know. Maybe it's a red herring. This place gets weirder by the minute. I need a drink. You wouldn't happen to have any Dutch courage in one of your pockets, would you?" I remembered the flask in my backpack and snapped my fingers. "Hold on, I think I got this one." I dug around and found the flask containing the strange spirits. I unscrewed the cap and took a swig. "Whoa. I don't have a clue what this stuff is." I handed it to Buzz.

He took a swig. "It ain't alcohol, but it is making me feel slightly tight."

We both smacked our tongues around in our mouths and blinked a bit. "Tastes like someone stuck a potted plant in a blender," I said.

"With some creme de menthe."

"Here's mud in your eye." I took another swig.

"Don't bogart that," Buzz said. He took the flask from me and drank some more, wiping his mouth with the back of his hand. He handed it back. I screwed the lid back on and put it away. "Wish I had my ballcap."

I took off the Dodgers hat and placed it on his head. It was slightly large, but fit him surprisingly well. "Meant to ask you about this. Is this the first mate's hat? Because I always took you to be a Cubs fan."

"The Cubs? Damn your eyes, Pepper!"

"Just kidding. Calm down. You know the Sox do their spring training in Sarasota. So this is the First Mate's cap?"

"Yeah, it's his."

"Almost had to take him down into the hold and beat some sense into him when he got wise to our plan, but the Soviets put the kibosh on that by showing up just in time."

"What the hell happened after the ship was hit?"

"Almost everyone got off in time. My team pulled the rest out of the drink, save for you and that cook."

"He's dead. Eaten by sharks, and not a moment too soon."

"We had one of our subs trailing behind, and a fast frigate behind that. Got the crew onboard the frigate, and my boys on the sub. Picked up the signal from the XAD-53 and trailed it here to the island. Was mighty glad to see you were still alive, daddy-o. You seem a little itchy. You got the combat yips?"

"I'm worried about Heena. It seems like every time I take my eyes off her, someone kidnaps her."

"The women here! Bostick may be a crumb, but he

sure did father some sweethearts. That little one with the pouty face? I want to feed her a chocolate chip cookie the size of a manhole cover. Can't even explain the urge."

"That's Judy, Toshiro's gal. There's another couple of tiny ones back at the village named Irene and Louise who do nothing but smile. I figure the little shrimps have the same ma. I hope you got some good shipmates on your team, because if they break any of these dolls' hearts, I'll have to knock their blocks off."

"Amen, brother! I'll whip my own men if it comes to that."

"Say, do you feel a bit strange? Speaking of itchy."

"Kinda tingly."

"Must be that stuff out of the flask. I feel… stronger."

"Me, too. I can't explain how I do, but I do. Say, didn't you have a bruise on your jaw a minute ago?"

We heard the crack of one of the Mausers and quit our gabbing.

Firefight!

"Deadeye dick!" Toshiro shouted. The two of them hopped up out of their trench and sprinted toward the next set of trenches.

We saw them down there, clear as day. It had to be a platoon of Soviet troops, all wearing helmets, olive drab choker tunics with shoulder boards, tan pants, knee-high black boots, ruck sacks, and toting AK-47's. A medic was helping the downed man.

We fired our pistols down at them, and they took cover quickly. Soon enough, we heard the Mausers blasting away, and we took off running to our next trench and hopped in.

The Soviets spread out a bit and started advancing up the hill in military fashion. There were too many of them to stop with a pair of pistols and bolt action rifles. I fired and hit a man in the shoulder. The 9-mm round didn't exactly kill him. Buzz had more luck and downed two men in five seconds. Hiro and Toshiro each downed a man as well. The medic was busy now, patching up the soldiers. They were 25 yards away and closing.

"What I wouldn't give for a grenade right now," Buzz said, snapping in a new magazine.

Hiro and Toshiro fell back again. Once they started firing, we did the same. We were almost at the crest of the hill.

"Russische Schweine!" we heard behind us. It was the Oberleutnant, his white linen suit wet with fresh blood, holding a couple of cans of knockout gas. He pitched one to our left and another to our right. We ducked and held our breath, knowing how potent it was. A round cracked through his right collarbone and he fell and rolled into our trench. Buzz and I caught him and laid him gently down. "I'm inclined to do stupid things in the heat of battle, Herr Russo," he said. He laughed a bit. "Er, *Russ*."

"You're not a coward, Otto. You were just too good to be a Nazi," I said.

He smiled at that, closed his eyes and died.

Down the hill, we saw two squads worth of Russians staggering around drunkenly, leaning against trees. We picked off ten of them quickly between the four of us, as the other men passed out and fell to the ground, some rolling as they fell. That left about 14 men with automatic weapons. We were still severely outgunned. They advanced up the hill with a renewed sense of mission.

The Reds clicked the Kalashnikov's over to full auto and rained bullets around us, splintering palm trees, killing several squawking multi-colored birds whose carcasses fell down amongst us, a 15-foot-long green-and-black striped snake thudded into the ground in front of us and rolled down the hill, wrapping itself around a bush in its death throes. The continuous stream of bullets tossed the rich volcanic soil upward, and finally hit Toshiro, who through all this continued to fire dutifully at the Russians one round at a time from the Mauser. He dropped his weapon, clutched his chest and fell into his hole. Hiro continued firing until he, too, was shot. With only pistols on our side now, Buzz and I ducked into the hole.

Buzz grabbed his left bicep with his right hand. Blood poured between his fingers like he was squeezing a tomato in his fist. "I'm fine," he said unconvincingly.

The bullets stopped flying. We heard the Soviets stomp up the hill, rustling the vegetation.

Colonel Comrade and his Commie Thugs!

"Is that you, Comrade Pepper? I think it is!" a heavily accented voice called out.

The lid to our hole was flung open, revealing ten enraged soldiers pointing automatic weapons at us. We tossed our pistols out, and then Buzz went back to holding his bicep. The colonel stepped between a pair of his men, their jaws clenched whitely, sweat dripping off all of them in great sheets. The colonel wore a brown tunic, black jodhpurs, black jackboots, a pair of long, brown-leather gauntlets, and an olive drab officer's hat with a red star affixed to the front of it. He didn't even have his weapon drawn. He stood smiling down at us, his face a contour map of occupied Europe, with moles supplying the hills and his eyes two ice-blue, oxygen-free lakes.

"I'm not your comrade, colonel!" Buzz replied. "I'm nobody's comrade!"

"I thought *we* were comrades," I said.

"Not in front of the commies!" Buzz snapped.

"Now this game has gone on long enough," the colonel said, tsk-tsking at us like we were naughty children. He took off one of the gauntlets and smacked it across the side of Buzz's head, knocking the Dodgers hat off him and onto the corpse of the former Nazi sharing the hole with us. "It's time to tell us a few things. First, how do you Americans control the volcano? Hmm? Yes? Does it have something to do with the dead German next to you? Is it Nazi science? And secondly, where is the XAD-53?"

"Do you honestly expect us to talk?" I asked him.

He sighed. "My men are very angry. You managed to kill half of them with a pair of ragged Japanese soldiers armed with bolt-action rifles, some sleeping gas, and two pistols. If I give them the word, they will tear you apart. Now stand up, if you please. And slowly."

We stood up carefully, still in the hole, and the Soviet troops kept the barrels of their weapons aimed at our mid-sections as we did so.

Without warning, a flying fox came zipping through, slammed into the colonel, knocking him down, and continued on its way. This happened so suddenly that the Soviet troops leapt backwards, away from the colonel, and lost their footing.

"Now!" I heard Dottie shout from above, the gals trilling out their war cry, and 11 bamboo spears zinged out, striking all 11 troops, including the colonel, each squarely in the chest. The soldiers sank to their knees and then slumped to the ground on their sides, their eyes and mouths wide in disbelief. Buzz leapt up and grabbed an AK-47, and I did likewise, but it was a worthless gesture. All 11 men were dead, or about to be.

"Comrade Stalin?" the colonel murmured, before the

light left his airless blue eyes for good.

Extraordinary Measures!

A pair of Navy F9F Panthers zipped overhead at treetop level wingtip-to-wingtip, split ways and zoomed past the steaming volcano in the distance.

A Cessna Cub with Navy insignia on it fluttered high above, ejected a skydiver, and a single parachute popped open a few hundred feet above the treetops.

"Right on time," Buzz said, shading his eyes against the relentless sun. Dottie plopped his cap on his head and kissed the little frogman on the lips. I picked up my Dodgers cap and took a wistful look at the dead former Nazi. I wished I could have gotten to know him better, but the way he died told me volumes about the kind of man he actually was.

I looked at Buzz's arm. "You're not bleeding anymore."

He lifted the sleeve of his Navy t-shirt and there was barely a scratch there. "That's odd," he said.

The 11 sisters descended from the trees and from parted bushes and stood gloriously around us. I'd nearly forgotten how intoxicating it was to be around so much beauty. Heena ran over to me quickly and we embraced. We heard a wailing coming from the opposite trench. Ruby and Judy were there, crouched over their men, shaking and hugging their limp bodies.

And then Ruby and Judy and the girls did something extraordinary.

Island Go-Juice Saves Gallant Soldiers!

We ran over to see if we could help the two prostrate soldiers, but I feared the worst.

Ruby leaned over Hiro, sealed her lips on his and blew

breath into his body. His chest rose and fell as she did so, but his wounds seemed too grievous. Red blood spread from the middle of his chest.

Toshiro was in the same state, his shirt bloody. A blood bubble popped in his open lips.

Judy suddenly pulled his bayonet from the scabbard, wrapped her hand around it, and pulled.

"Judy, no!" I heard myself shout. I thought she was trying to kill herself. But that wasn't the case.

She placed her bloody hand over one of the wounds in his chest and let her blood seep in for a moment. Then she did it for the other wound. Strangely, the color was returning to his face.

Hiro coughed and tried to sit up for a moment, but Ruby pushed him back down. "Not yet," she said.

She and Judy stood up and joined hands with their sisters. They formed a circle around the two soldiers, and slowly walked around them, singing, solemnly:

The moon belongs to everyone

The best things in life are free,

The stars belong to everyone

They gleam there for you and me.

The volcano kicked up again with a rumble. It was a gentle eruption, almost like a thunderclap two towns away. No rock ejected this time, only a spray of ash, which the wind carried directly overhead until it rained down upon us. The ash glowed green like a radium clock's hands—the same green color as the liquor that Buzz and I had swallowed down before the firefight. I snapped my fingers. "Dang me!" I shouted. "They oughta get a rope and hang me!" I ran back to the trench, retrieved my bag, and shook the liquor. It was about half-full. "Excuse me ladies," I said, and ducked between Franny and Lizzie, who didn't seem to mind the interruption of their ritual, if that was what you would call it.

I unscrewed the cap and poured a dollop in Hiro's mouth.

The girls stopped. "What is that?" Ruby demanded.

"Some sort of island go-juice!" I said. "Look at Buzz's arm."

"What about it?" Dottie said. Buzz showed off the arm. It was bloodstained, but there was no longer a wound there.

"He got shot in that arm."

I ran over to Toshiro and poured some in his mouth. He immediately sat bolt upright, swallowed, and looked at me. "Russo-san!" He plopped back down.

The girl circle broke up and the volcano stopped rumbling. A moment later, the sun peeked through the sparkling dark cloud above us and the rain of ash ceased.

I unbuttoned Toshiro's shirt and we watched as his wounds faded away. His eyes blinked open and he called out, "Ruby, baby!" She bent down and took him in her arms, and then planted kisses all over his face.

Toshiro was having a similar revival. We pulled the two soldiers out of their hole. They sat up and seemed fine for two men who were dying of bullet wounds only moments before.

I handed Hiro the flask and he took another drink. He handed it over to Toshiro, who did likewise. All of the girls descended on the two men and each laid a kiss on the two of them. I don't think I've ever seen two happier men in my life. The girls were thrilled, too.

I saw Irene out of the corner of my eye, standing just outside the critical mass of her sisters. She beamed at me. Louise stood behind her slightly taller sister.

"Holy mackerel, more tiny dames!" Buzz said. "You're cute as buttons. What's your names?"

"Ask *him*," she said, pointing at me.

"Irene," I said. "Her name's Irene. And the one behind her is Louise."

The Chief Discovers a New Euphemism!

While all this was going on, a large man sauntered up like he was approaching us on a street corner back on the block. Maybe he was going to show us a selection of watches in a briefcase, or challenge us to a game of three-card monte. "How y'doin', L-T?" He snapped off a salute, which Buzz quickly returned.

"Fair to middlin', Chief," Buzz replied. "Chief Jack O'Neill, meet Russ Russo. He killed his fair share of Russians today."

We shook hands. O'Neill had a good, Midwestern double-pumper of a handshake. I liked him right away.

Chief Jack O'Neill was a tall, barrel-chested cuss, dressed head-to-shins in khaki, an anchor on each collar of his shirt and one on his piss-cutter. A pair of spit-shined black jumpboots were laced on his enormous feet, his trousers bloused above them. He produced a thermos of coffee from a map bag slung across his body, along with a porcelain mug with chief's anchors on it. He poured himself a cup of joe without offering us any, set the thermos down on a tree stump, and then produced a pack of smokes from his bag and shook one out for the three of us.

The pack was green, so I asked him if they were menthols.

"Menthols?" he roared. "I'd kill a man with my bare hands if he offered me menthols!" Turned out they were Luckies that he bought at the Navy Exchange.

I lit all the cigarettes with my Zippo, which O'Neill squinted at suspiciously.

"Army man, eh?" he said.

"During the war. I'm in the merchant marine now," I said.

"That's all right then. I had to forgive the L-T for his former Army proclivities, and I guess I'll do the same for you," he said.

"That's a familiar accent you got there. Where're you from?"

"Cicero," he said.

"It's like a Chicago hometown reunion party in this place. I grew up on the near southside. My pop still runs a butcher shop there."

"Ah, I miss Italian beef," O'Neill said, his eyes getting misty. "And a cold Old Style to go along with it. What's with the Dodgers hat?"

"Don't pay any attention to it. I'm a Sox fan all the way."

He squinted suspiciously at me again. "Just when I was beginning to like you. Cubs," he said, jerking a meaty thumb at his midsection, the cigarette taking a jaunty upturn in his kisser. He plucked out the cigarette and took a swig of his coffee. "It's gettin' cold." He looked around and noticed all the beautiful half-naked women. "Christ almighty, look at these dishes. Here I was worried about you like an old mother hen, L-T, and you been sittin' pretty all this time."

We finished our smokes almost simultaneously and flicked the butts onto the ground.

Sandy nearly leapt over the top of Irene and Louise,

landed like a ballerina on her tiptoes, her blond hair and bountiful breasts bouncing, and walked around the chief, patting him like he was a prize steer at a cattle auction.

"Friendly, aren't they?" O'Neill said, standing there and taking it.

"Shipmate, you don't know the half of it," Buzz said.

"I call him!" Sandy shouted to the other girls. There was a little grumbling amongst the single girls.

"Call me anything but late for dinner," O'Neill said.

She pinched his potato-shaped nose, her eyes lighting up. "You like to eat, I can see that."

"Sister, I like anything you like."

"I'm Sandy. Maybe later I'll let you wash my feet."

"Is that one of them, uh... euphemisms?" O'Neill asked.

"I've been wondering about this feet-washing obsession myself," Buzz said. "Maybe our esteemed colleague in the merchant marine can put our minds to rest."

"I happily washed Heena's feet. Which was followed by a wedding feast. These gals may sound like they're from the Midwest, but they have their own customs here, believe you me."

"Which one's Heena?" O'Neill asked, right before Sandy grabbed his ears, and pulled him in for a long kiss. He came out of the kiss gasping for air. "On the other hand—" And Sandy kissed him again, this time longer. He dropped the coffee mug as his arms wrapped around her. They finished again and O'Neill looked half-drunk. "Ahh. We were talkin' about something?"

"Washing my feet," Sandy said, running her hands up and down his chest.

"I can do that. Name's Jack, by the way."

Heena slipped up next to me and my arm automatically draped itself over her shoulders. I looked down at her, and immediately became immersed in her twinkling blue-green and gold eyes. "That face!" I said aloud.

We heard some groans coming from downhill, like drunk men recovering from a bar fight gone horribly wrong.

"Excuse me," O'Neill said. To Sandy: "Be right back, darlin'! Don't go nowhere."

He stomped down the hill and casually cracked each Russian across the jaw, snatched their weapons and slung them on his non-punching arm.

Sandy bubbled watching him. "He's burly!" She clapped her hands excitedly.

"Yah! You got a good one. You'll have hu-u-uge bay-bees with him!" Heena said. She rubbed her own belly and looked up at me longingly. My knees trembled.

A half-dozen Navy frogmen suddenly appeared out of the woods carrying Thompson machine guns, all dressed identically to Buzz, but with blue ballcaps, all of them vaguely familiar from the *Mother's Mercy*.

"Chief! Chief!" they shouted down to O'Neill.

"Where the hell have you bums been?"

"Chief!" they shouted. "Chief! Chief!"

"Get your asses down here and secure these prisoners!"

"Secure the prisoners, aye, chief!" they shouted and trotted down, but not before leering at the girls, and snapping off quick salutes to Buzz.

That Old Fatty is Gonna Be Trouble!

With the prisoners secured and lined up, we were ready to march back to the village. One of the frogmen sauntered up to Buzz and said, "We headed back to that village, sir?" His voice was a tired croak.

"Yes, Mitch. We're heading back there."

"Cuz we left our gear there with some slick old fatty and his stick boy son. He was American, as was the boy, so we figured we could trust'm." Mitch took off his blue ballcap and ran his fingers over his slicked hair. He replaced the ballcap. He gazed around the jungle with drooping eyes.

"Anything else?" Buzz asked him.

"Just a feeling, sir."

"Out with it."

"That old fatty is gonna be trouble."

"Don't say that too loud around these gals. That tubbo is their father. That will be all."

"Aye, sir." Mitch sauntered off in an unexcited fashion. Louise slipped up to him. She was barely above waist-high to Mitch, who was about my height. He leaned down and listened to her talk and a moment later she leapt up onto his back for a piggyback ride to the village.

"They don't waste any time, these chickadees," Buzz said.

"They never learned to be coy isolated out on this island," I said. "I find them all to be charmingly direct."

"I keep thinking about washing Dottie's feet. It seems like a fair proposition. I think there's a chaplain aboard USS *Forrestal*, too, so we can all get hitched legal-like to these delightful dames if we so please."

"Like we have any say in it."

"True enough."

"I already consider Heena to be my wife, so I might as well get the legal part over with." At my own mention of her name, I peered nervously around and saw her helping Toshiro to his feet. Judy hugged and squeezed him tight. Heena gave him a peck on the cheek and then saw me watching her and smiled beatifically and waved. As usual, my knees nearly gave out just looking at her.

Marching Orders!

The frogmen all crowded around Buzz and took a knee, with only O'Neill standing. I stood to one side. Mitch still had Louise on his back. Her feet had slipped under his pistol belt. Her arms were wrapped around his neck and her cheek was up against the back of his neck. She was so damned cute that I had to suppress an "aww." Hicks, a sailor with long black hair slicked into a pompadour and pouty lips, didn't. The *aww* came out of him in a lascivious manner. Then he pinched her cheek.

Mitch gave him a proprietary look, and Hicks backed off a bit. "Hey, man. Didn't mean to touch your little lady," he said in a Mississippi drawl.

"See that you avoid it in the future," Mitch said.

Tank and Elroy were a pair of blonde California surfers with perfect straight white teeth. Tank had the GRC-109 radio. Elroy carried a musette bag with a red cross on it. They performed an elaborate handshake ritual. "You bring your board?" Tank asked.

"You know it," Elroy said. "Stowed onboard *Forrestal* with our other gear. Totally gonna surf the beach where we came ashore."

"R&R!" Tank said. They shook hands in another elaborate way.

Scrimshaw wore a pair of black-rimmed glasses held on by rubberbands around the back of his head. A sketchpad was shoved in the back of his shorts, and a soft pencil stuck out of his pocket. His hair was almost as out-of-regs as Hicks', a long brown mop, combed off his ears. He had a mustache that clearly needed trimming, too.

Hondo was, amongst all these tough guys, the roughest looking of them all. He had red hair cut into a severe bristle, a long, dark scar across his cheek, and a look of pure murder in his eyes.

The Soviet prisoners were sitting in a tight circle, guarded by Hiro and Toshiro, who seemed more hale and hearty in their post-injury life than they had previously, the only sign that anything had happened to them being their bloody shirts.

Hiro showed Ruby how to fire the AK-47, the switches and the sights.

"Like this?" she asked, and snapped out the retractable stock, tucked it into her shoulder, aimed and shot a coconut off a tree. The coconut hit the ground and split perfectly in half.

The Soviets went from sullen to impressed in one second flat.

Hiro said, "I love you."

Ruby said, "You better."

All of the sailors were watching, and then turned and looked at Buzz, who said, "So you may have noticed that the native population consists of some mighty impressive ladies. If you break any of their hearts, I don't think I have to tell you the consequences."

"No, sir!" they all barked out.

"That said, if one of these gals 'calls' you, feel free to do what your heart tells you."

"Calls us, aye, sir!" they chimed back at him.

"We're going to follow the trail to the native village, lock those Soviets up, and wait for the task force to arrive. I understand Admiral Stump himself is coming ashore."

Tank nodded in the affirmative and patted the radio.

"Let's move out."

"Move out, aye, sir!"

Most of the AK-47's were pitched into one of the hidey-holes, and covered back over. The dead Soviets were lined up, ready for mortuary affairs when they came ashore with the Fleet.

The Navy Works Fast!

O'Neill led the way, with Sandy holding onto his arm. She had a grip on him like an iceman's tongs. We came upon his parachute hanging in a tree. A leather football helmet was next to the chute. Jack bunched up his parachute and handed it to Sandy. "Wedding dress," he attempted to say nonchalantly, but the wobble in his voice gave the salty chief away.

"You are so… *burly!*" she enthused, hugging her future dress against herself.

"I think you left a mark on my arm," he said, shaking the feeling back into it.

Toshiro and Judy walked up and Toshiro nearly lost his mind over the football helmet. "Red Grange!" he shouted, and put it on his head. We all laughed.

"I like this guy," O'Neill said.

"Papa Bear Halas!"

"I'm liking him better and better. You hang onto that helmet."

I heard a rough chuckle behind us, turned and saw Louise nibbling on Mitch's ear, her arms cinched tightly around his thick neck. An unaccustomed smile broke out on his face. "Cut it out," he said, not meaning it.

There was a lot of pairing off. Buzz wasn't kidding. This was pretty fast, even for the Navy.

I stood with Heena, gently stroking her back, watching each couple stroll past. First Mitch and Louise, a definite odd couple. Then came Gloria and Scrimshaw, followed by Betty and Hicks. Good matches, my brain told me. Then came Tank and Franny alongside Elroy and Lizzie. More sense. The coppertone twins with the Coppertone twins.

The Soviet troops came up behind, their hands on their heads, followed by Hondo, who held a Thompson on them. Behind him was Irene, following him by about five feet, walking in an almost-prance. I didn't have a lot of hope for that particular pairing. Even the bright sunshine of her disposition couldn't possibly melt a rage like that, I thought.

They were all up ahead. Irene turned and cast a smiling gaze back at us and disappeared around the bend.

"Why—?" Heena started to ask, and then she got her answer. I kissed her longingly and deeply. "Russo!" she gasped afterward, fanning her hands at her face. She broke away from me and gathered some palm fronds, took off her pretty kerchief-turned-skirt and placed it down on the frond bed. I took off my shirt and undershirt. I spread out the undershirt so we wouldn't ruin her skirt. She laid on her back and beckoned me to join her.

Procreation and the *Encyclopedia Brittanica!*

Afterwards, as I pulled on my clothes and she reknotted her skirt, I said, "I always want it to be like this."

"Yah, it will be, Russo. Try to enjoy the moment." She wiped herself with my white undershirt and tossed it into the jungle. She painted a word picture of us in fifty years, sitting outside our hut enjoying our children, and their children, and their children. "All that life," she concluded. "So much happiness! I hope we just made our first baby. The *Encyclopedia Brittanica* was kinda vague on the process, don'tcha know."

"I think we nailed the process pretty good," I said.

We kissed and then held each other surrounded by the jungle and its noises for a long moment.

"We'd better catch up," Heena said. "It'll be getting dark soon."

The Papa Wally Plan!

We caught up with the procession as we neared the village. Papa Wally stood next to his only male progeny, both of them with a cat-who-swallowed-the-canary look on their conniving faces. The boy had discovered a pair of scissors at some point, and had trimmed his hair down to 1950's standards, slicked it up just like Hicks', with a ducktail in the back for good measure. They were both dressed in finery, and had even come up with a pair of pants for them each and dress shoes, though Wally Junior's were big enough that they looked like clown shoes on him.

As the Navy men approached, each of the Wallys proffered a hand in greeting, which was shaken by the men as they passed. "Howyadoin', howyadoin'," the two Wallys asked each of them. "Real good! Real good!"

Another boar was in the pit, smoking, and a bonfire had been prepared for us. I was the last one to shake Papa Wally's and Wally Junior's hands. The twiggy little teen gave me a pretty good bonecrusher. He must have been working on it for a while.

"You ready for something to eat?" Papa Wally asked. "Been roasting that pig all day long, don'tcha know."

"Smells wonderful," I said.

"You been having some adventures, sweet pea?" he asked Heena.

"Yah, we been having a crazy time. The monkeys are all dead."

"I noticed some Russians amongst you, too."

"Mondo blew up their boat," Heena said.

"Sure he did, honey pie," Papa Wally said solicitously. He and Wally Junior shared an amused look. "You run along and help the other girls prepare the big feast. Man talk."

"Oh," she said, looking confused. "Um. Sure." She kissed me and stroked my cheek for a moment.

"Get outta here!" Wally Junior said. "Scram! Man talk!"

I nearly punched the little creep, but held back.

"Be nice to your sister, for cripe's sake," Papa Wally said, stroking his long whiskers.

"Sorry, Heena," Wally Junior said, not looking at all chastised.

"Guh," Heena went, rolling her eyes. "I'm glad all men aren't like you." She winked at me, spun on her lovely heel and trotted off in search of her sisters.

"So, the Navy is headed this way? Am I right? And we all get to go back to civilization?" Papa Wally asked.

"That's my understanding. I'm guessing from your tone that you're planning on taking a hike. Not gonna be the major-domo anymore?"

"You could say that," Wally Junior said. "Not around here, leastways. Heh-heh!"

"Heh-heh," Papa Wally went.

"Heh-heh," Wally Junior went.

"Thing is, there's a box I need brought up. Heavy box. Filled with what you might want to call precious metal. And as my best and favorite son-in-law, I figured you'd want first shot at it."

"At the moment, I'm your only son-in-law. Not

interested."

"Come now! We can make it worth your while," Papa Wally said. "Show him what you've got in the sack, fruit of my loins."

Wally Junior untied a sack the size of a grocery bag and exposed the contents in front of me. "Did a little snorkeling today with that Navy equipment. Took me a few minutes to figure it out. Heh-heh!"

I peered in the sack and saw dozens of perfect white pearls the size of Kix cereal.

"Lookee there, friend! Plenty more where that came from. Enough to satisfy all of your wildest desires!" Papa Wally said. He rubbed his belly and grinned at me.

"Wildest desires!" Wally Junior said, slapping his raised knee.

"I have everything I need. I have Heena."

"But think of what you could give her. With these pearls, you could buy her a palace filled with servants! You think someone of her coloration is going to do well back in America? She's as dark as a negro! The two of you will need real folding money to merely survive life in the United States—to avoid getting lynched."

"Who says we're going back?"

"You don't intend to stay *here*, do you, when you could take this treasure and live life as a rich man with your beautiful bride? Hell, you could live in Connecticut with money like this! Sure, your darkie children wouldn't be allowed in the country club—"

"Connecticut!" Wally Junior piped in.

"The boy here, I've intentionally kept out of the sun. He's my progeny, and will live life as a white man."

"Caucasian!" Wally Junior said, thumping his chest.

"I fully intend to stay here with Heena and make a life with her, surrounded by our children. I love her too much to take her away from this place."

"You're a fool! A damned fool!" Papa Wally roared.

"Damned fool!" Wally Junior agreed. "Pumpkin head! Nitwit! Turkey gobbler!"

"I've been waiting to get away from here for decades, to get back to real life," Papa Wally continued. "And now that Capone is dead, and the statute of limitations has passed, I can finally go home to Wisconsin, buy a mansion, live the life I deserve. Maybe get back into business."

"The business of America is business!" Wally Junior said.

"We're natural empire builders, we Americans!"

"Manifest destiny!"

"I wouldn't tell Heena that if I were you. Pick up and go when the Fleet arrives tomorrow. Leave here and don't return. Take your pearls with you."

"And my treasure. Don't forget my treasure."

"It's our nut! To start up our business!"

"Neither one of you appear to be in any shape to pull a chest of gold out of the water."

"Fine," Papa Wally said. "I'm sure some other sap will be happy to pull that treasure up from the depths."

"Plenty of saps," Wally Junior agreed. "Navy boys. Saps!"

"Good luck with that," I said, but I didn't mean it. Not one word.

In the distance, Mondo Tiki agreed with me with a rumble and a belch of flames.

A God By Any Other Name!

I walked home to the hut, climbed the stairs, opened the door and found Heena in there. She'd washed her skirt and had it hanging on the clothesline, and had put on another grass skirt. She sat at the little vanity, combing her hair, her feet crossed at the ankles.

I pulled over a chair, sat behind her, gently took the comb from her, and continued combing her hair. She looked at me from the warped mirror, a worried smile on her face. "Are you going back to sea, Russo? Are you going to leave me sitting here like a weeping widow?"

"All the traveling I'll do from now on will be in your eyes."

"That's pretty darned corny, Russo. But I'll take it."

I put the comb down and wrapped my arms around her from behind. She broke my embrace, got up and sat down in my lap, her arm around my shoulders, and we conversed with each other in low voices. She told me about her mother, Luana, the last of the native women on the island, and how Luana told her the real stories of Maui Tiki. "Papa Wally called him 'Mondo,' so we did, too. I figured it was like all the names you got for your God. Jehovah, Yahweh, Hashem, Jesus... a god by any other name, and so forth.

Papa Wally's stories were almost like my ma's. I've read the Bible. God changes in there from story to story. He's angry, he's nice; he's paying attention, he isn't; he has a body, he don't."

"It seems like Mondo listens to you, unlike *my* God," I said with a tremolo of shaky rage.

She sighed. "You frighten me sometimes."

"I'm sorry."

The light dimmed outside. I told her about the war. I apologized to her for bringing the Cold War to her island, for making her and her sisters into killers.

"Yah, but it had to be done, Russo. They were threatening our men, don'tcha know. Can't have that."

"You'll see their eyes forever whenever you close yours."

"Yah, I know it. But it seems like small potatoes compared to losing you." She arched her eyebrows. "Hey, we're getting in pretty deep here! I got a better idea. Why don't we go for a soak before the big to-do?" She hopped up out of my lap and I stood up. My legs had fallen asleep, so I walked in circles for a moment until I shook the tingles. I took one of her hands in mine and kissed it on each side.

We walked out the door just as the sun dipped and disappeared. I grabbed a torch and lit it with my Zippo. We walked down the path, past the sugarcane fields, and into the jungle.

Canoodling Interrupted!

A little while later, we found ourselves at the spring. On the opposite side, we could see torches glowing, and other couples canoodling in the flickering torchlight. Apparently, the soak wasn't an original idea. Heena lifted up a rock and took out a bar of coconut soap. She pulled a string and her grass skirt rustled to the ground. "Shall we?" She stepped out of the skirt.

I planted the torch in the black sand. I sat down on the rock, untied my boots—which in the heat, humidity, sweat and use had stretched out to fit my feet perfectly—and quickly disrobed. Heena took my hand and pulled me into the cool, clear water. We soaped each other in the shallows. I put the soap back in the rock, and swam out to the center of the pool and played grab-ass with her for a while, splashing around, both of us giggling like children.

We were all interrupted by the grinding gears of a Willy's jeep as it pulled into the clearing opposite of us, where most of the couples were.

"Chief?" the sailors called out. "Chief? Chief?"

"What?" O'Neill roared, emerging from behind the waterfall with Sandy, both of them naked, and both freshly shorn from the face down. O'Neill wasn't completely naked. He'd left on his piss-cutter with the chief's anchor on it.

The jeep had small spotlights mounted on the back on a swivel. The light beamed around the site, illuminating the couples there—Mitch and Louise; Gloria and Scrimshaw; and Hicks and Betty.

I squinted through the bright light and saw the white flag mounted on the front. I thought at first it was the admiral, but a slight breeze revealed a blue K in the middle. It was my boss, or former boss, Old Man Konrath. "Any of you boys belong to me?" came the voice out of a loudspeaker. Old Man Konrath turned on a flashlight and stuck it under his chin like he was about to tell a stretcher around the campfire.

"Right here, sir!" I called out from the middle of the spring. The spotlight quickly turned in my direction, blinding me. I held a blocking hand in front of my eyes.

"Who's that?"

"Russell Russo, third mate and navigator aboard the former SS *Mother's Mercy*," I replied.

"Russo! We've been looking all over for you, chum!" The light extinguished and Old Man Konrath waded out in his clothes in the water. He was wearing a yachting outfit, complete with blue blazer, ascot and skipper's hat. He was up to his knees by the time we met. He shook my hand a bit limply, and slapped me on the arm. "You don't look the worse for wear, that's for sure!"

"Thank you, sir."

"Well, hell, put some clothes on and let's get you ready to go back to work."

"I don't think I'm going to do that, sir. I've given it a lot of thought, and I'd like to stay here with my bride."

Heena waded up and shook his hand, a good double-pumper, I noticed. "Nice to meetcha," she said. "That's some jalopy you got there."

"Er, thanks," Konrath said, drinking her in with his eyes. "Why don't you both get dressed and we can discuss this some more."

"You're welcome to come to our feast tonight," Heena said. "But my man stays wherever I stay. That's not negotiable."

"Who's wearing the pants around here, Russo?"

Konrath asked, a bit crossly. Then he looked down. "I guess neither one of you." He laughed. "Oh, hell! Who am I to stand in the way of love? Let's go chow down. I'll give you a ride in my jeep." He stuck his fingers in his mouth and whistled loudly. The floodlight turned back on, blinding me again.

"Hiya, Heena!" called a voice from the jeep.

Heena made a face. "Is that you, Art?"

"Sure is! Guess what? I have a career now! I'm a company man!"

"My men found these three gents wandering around on the beach this morning and brought them onboard for interrogation. They're wonderful bootlicks, and have no idea about money, so I put them under contract right away."

"I take it Marty and Les are in the jeep, too," I said.

"Yes, yes! They've already been civilized by missionaries, and seem to have no urges other than to please whoever happens to have the loudest voice. Which is almost always me."

"We want sex!" Les shouted. "Not necessarily right away."

"I told you lads I'd take you to a Reno brothel next week! Now shut your pie holes!"

"Yes, sir!" they all chimed together.

"Ahh, but do we have to wear these ties?" Marty asked. "So constricting!"

"You all wear ties! No exceptions!" Konrath leaned over to us. "Never found better servants in my life, even amongst the Mormons!"

"What's a Mormon?" Heena asked. She pinched her nose, closed her eyes, dunked into the water and bobbed back up, her body shimmering in the dense light from the jeep.

"Ahh!" the three lads went. "Do it again!" Marty shouted.

"Can you kill the light, sir?" I asked.

Konrath ran a thumb across his throat and the light went out.

O'Neill waded up. "So you're that Konrath guy, huh?"

"I am."

"Puh," he went contemptuously, and turned around, showing us his ass. He strode over to Sandy, tossed her over his shoulder, and went under the waterfall again.

"Burly!" Sandy called out. "So *burly*!"

To the Cave!

Konrath kicked Art, Les and Marty out of the jeep with instructions to walk to the village, and to keep their suits on. He'd dressed them up like three undertakers, in black suits, white shirts and black ties. Their hair was razored into a corporate look and Brylcreemed into place.

"Bespoke suits," Konrath said. "Always bring my tailor with me wherever I go for exigencies like this one. Turn around." The three lads turned around. "Now get to walking."

"Oww, these shoes!"

"Who invented shoes?"

"A madman, that's who."

"Don't take off any of that clothing! You're company men now!"

"Yes, sir!"

His driver was the former first mate of the *Mother's*

Mercy, Gil Elvgren, who was dressed in khakis. Heena and I had dressed. Elvgren took the opportunity to snatch the Dodger's hat off my head and stick it on his own. "I believe this is mine."

"Just keeping it warm for you, first," I said.

"Hell of a navigator you turned out to be."

"I don't know. I think I arrived at my destination, even if it wasn't by design." I helped Heena up into the back seat of the jeep and joined her there. Old Man Konrath sat shotgun. Elvgren turned on the headlights and burned rubber away from the spring. The frogmen and their prospective wives were preparing to leave.

We pulled pretty quickly into the village, where we met Hiro and Ruby, who were just getting ready to go. "Where're you headed, chum?" Konrath asked Hiro.

"To the cave," Hiro replied. "To convince the rest of my soldiers to come quietly."

"Sounds good," Konrath said, hopping out of the jeep. "Take my spot. Mister Elvgren will drive you up there."

"If you don't mind, I'll go with him," I said.

"Me, too," Heena said, holding tight onto my arm. The wind had dried out her hair, and she looked more lovely that ever in the torchlight of the village. Ruby slipped in next to her.

"I'll go talk with the chief in this village. He got a name?" Konrath asked.

"Wally Bostick," I said.

"Wally Bostick! *The* Wally Bostick? He and I go way back!"

"Sir?"

"Before the Great War, he was my best salesman for Konrath's Kure, a nostrum that made me my first fortune. Here, have a bottle!" He tossed it over to me. It was a glass bottle with green liquid in it. I popped it open and tasted the liquid. It was much like the stuff that I'd fed Hiro and Toshiro to revive them, though something essential was missing. I handed it to Heena.

"Smells like Papa Wally's special homebrew," she said. She took a sip and smacked her lips. "Minus the togo root."

"That's what I fed to Hiro and Toshiro," I said.

"Yah, it heals wounds. Keeps y'regular, too, don'tcha know. Been takin' it since I was a tiny girl, about yay-high."

"Healed them?" Konrath said.

"This man here," I said, slapping Hiro on the back, "was at death's door just hours ago. I'd suggest you find ol' Wally and get him to point out the togo root. You may have another fortune to make, sir."

"I'm liking this island more and more, chum!" Konrath hurried toward the bonfire, which was growing.

"Hiro, you'll have to show us the way," I said. I showed him the loudspeaker and the microphone as we drove, with Hiro pointing out the way through the jungle, and the Willy's jeep flat out conquering it. Ruby leaned over the seat, her hands on Hiro's shoulders.

I looked over at Heena. This felt like a great night. As it turned out, it wasn't.

Honor!

Outside the cave, Hiro spoke through the loudspeaker. His voice was filled with feeling. He pleaded. He begged. But no response came from the cave. Not a peep.

I turned on the big light and aimed it in there. I made out the bodies with the bayonets sticking out of their bellies.

"Heena! Don't look!" I said to her, but it was too late. I placed my hand over her eyes. She buried her face in my chest, and I held her tight.

Hiro slowly got up from his seat and staggered over to them. He fell to his knees in front of cave and wept loudly. Ruby got out of the jeep, but stood next to it. Her hands covered her mouth.

"Jesus Christ," Elvgren said. "Why?"

"Honor!" Hiro shouted out in reply, like he couldn't believe the word coming out of his mouth. "Honor!" He slowly walked back toward us, his face wracked in the pain of loss, his cheeks stained with tears. He held out a note written in Kanji. "They committed seppuku after seeing the American airplanes, the ones without props that went very fast. They know. They knew." He drew his own bayonet.

"No!" I shouted. "Don't do it, Hiro! Think of Ruby!"

Ruby started to run toward him.

He snapped the rusty bayonet in half over his knee and tossed it in the jungle. "I say, 'fuck honor!'" Ruby wrapped her arms around the soldier.

I turned off the light.

Admiral Bud Stump Arrives!

We drove in solemn silence back to the village, Hiro sitting in his seat as still as a statue. He finally said, "They are all dead." Ruby got out of the jeep took him by the hand and led him away. We didn't see the two of them the rest of the night.

We did see a helicopter near the fire, adorned with four stars and Navy decals. It could only be Admiral Bud Stump, Commander-in-Chief, Pacific Fleet. Soon enough, we saw him, tall and spindly, wearing his khaki's and a piss-cutter with four stars. His aide and the helo pilot followed him around while he spoke with Lt. Pepper, who had apparently finished debriefing him. I overheard that the Soviet soldiers had already been evacuated to the *Forrestal*, which was just off the coast in deep waters.

Wally Junior started beating on a set of bongos, and we all made our way to the fire, where Admiral Stump took his place in the seat of honor on the dais, with Papa Wally sitting on one side and Old Man Konrath on the other. I was happy to sit in the sand next to my girl this time, just another lucky fellow. Everyone but Ruby and Hiro sat around the fire, and we each had a leaf covered over with bananas, pork, papaya, and other choice morsels in front of us. We all also had a coconut shell filled with Papa Wally's deadly rum. Despite all of the death we'd witnessed that day, the mood turned festive quickly.

"I'm so hungry I could eat a horse and chase the rider!" Chief O'Neill shouted, to laughter and applause.

"A toast," Admiral Stump said, standing up. We all stood up with him and held our coconut halves filled with potent rum before us. "To these fine and, quite frankly, ravishing girls who saved our bacon!"

"To the girls!" all the gents shouted at once. We all drank.

Dottie called out, "And a toast to the boys. You ain't half-bad either!"

"To the boys!" the girls shouted at once. We all drank again.

"You make this carburetor cleaner yourself?" Admiral Stump asked Papa Wally.

"The boy helped," he said, nodding at Wally Junior.

"Handsome lad," the admiral said.

"Thanks, fella," the little creep said, to raucous laughter.

Raising the Kids Right!

We ate for a while, with Sandy continually jumping up to get the Chief more food. She was fascinated by how much he was stuffing down his throat. "Look at him *eat!*" she kept saying, practically glowing while he stuffed his mighty maw. "Oh, he can sure put it away!" She clapped her hands in excitement. "We're gonna have *big* babies!"

"You know it," O'Neill said in between bites. "Chester Nimitz O'Neill. First boy."

Tank and Elroy were running around the bonfire with Franny and Lizzie standing on their shoulders, pretending they were surfing.

Dottie and Buzz disappeared for a moment, and then returned with the XAD-53, which they placed on the ground in front of Admiral Stump. The admiral tapped the remains out of his pipe with a grin, his legs crossed, while Papa Wally spoke in one ear and Old Man Konrath spoke in the other.

Gloria and Scrimshaw had a huge sheet of paper in front of them, onto which they'd drawn a map of the island, complete with trees, sugar cane, mountains, and our village and the various sites on the other side of the island. I watched as Gloria slowly took off Scrimshaw's glasses and placed them on her own face. She played with his mustache a bit, peering through the cheaters.

Toshiro and Judy sat near us, and I heard her consoling him over the loss of his compatriots.

Mitch and Louise were off to the side, nearly the least likely of all the pairs at the fire. They appeared to be in deep conversation, sitting crosslegged facing each other, the lumpen palooka and the princess-like doll.

Then there was Irene, who I could have easily fallen in love with, with her compassionate nature, sitting next to Hondo, who looked like he'd swallowed a box of ten-penny nails. They sat on our left, with Hondo sullenly chewing on his pork, his elbows jutted out, radiating anger. He was the only one of the enlisted men—other than the Chief—who seemed old enough to have fought in the war. The island was dredging up some sort of bitterness for him. That much was certain. Hondo finished his meal and tossed the leaf into the fire. He watched it burn. Irene stood up and tapped him on the shoulder. He turned and looked at her. She leaned in and whispered in his ear through a cupped hand for what seemed like a full two minutes. Whatever she said threw cold water upon the inferno of his rage. His face softened and he blinked for a moment. "I'm sorry," he said to her, in a voice that sounded like it had been roughened by broken glass. "I've been cruel."

She ran her finger along the scar on his face. "There's nothing to be sorry about," she said. Hondo stood up and the two of them walked off toward the huts silently together.

"How do you like that?" Heena asked, watching them along with me.

"I'm a big believer in Mondo," I said. "We're gonna raise our kids right. Mondo all the way."

"I know you're kidding," she said, rubbing my arm.

"Not even half-kidding," I said. "Not even a quarter kidding." I was a little drunk. I stood up and raised my coconut. "To Mondo Tiki, the god of this island! May his benevolent hand guide us all to a bright future, as he as guided us all together!"

"Here, here!" O'Neill said, leaping to his feet. "To by-god Mondo! He's some kinda all right!"

"To Mondo! Here's mud in your eye!" Buzz shouted, raising his coconut as well. Soon, all the men left around the fire, even the Admiral, were toasting the volcano god.

Mondo rumbled his approval.

The only men left seated were Papa Wally and Wally Junior. They had a smirky look on their faces like we were suckers ready for fleecing.

Before I could take that in completely, Hicks and Betty stood together and sang a duet, their voices blending beautifully, as Betty plucked out the melody on her ukulele.

Sometimes I wonder why I spend

The lonely nights

Dreaming of a song.

The melody haunts my reverie

And I am once again with you.

When our love was new, and each kiss an inspiration.

But that was long ago, and now my consolation

Is in the stardust of a song.

Taboo!

In the morning, we awoke curled up next to the fire. Only the admiral had decided to take lodging. Old Man Konrath and Papa Wally sat next to each other on the little stage plotting. I walked over and asked them what the plan was.

"Mr. Konrath here has generously accepted my proposition to excavate my treasure from the pearl beds in exchange for the formula to my enervating drink," Papa Wally said.

"It's the drink that cures!" Wally Junior said, hopping up from behind the two men, his face now frozen in the rictus of a perma-smirk.

"Pearl beds!" Heena said, standing behind me. "Did I hear that right? Pearl beds? You know it's taboo to go in the pearl beds, Papa Wally!" She turned around and shouted out, "Did you hear that, girls?"

"Hear what?" Dottie asked, rubbing the sleep out of her eyes.

"Papa Wally and this Konrath fella are going to go diving in the pearl beds!" Heena said.

Upon hearing this, she shook Buzz awake and helped him up. "Hey, bud. That Konrath joker wants to go diving in the pearl beds."

"So?"

"It's taboo, and Mondo don't like it. Not one bit," she said.

Sandy and O'Neill were up and she elbowed him in the ribs. "Mondo don't like it," she repeated to him.

"Yeah, I got that," O'Neill said. To Konrath he said, "Stop making Mondo angry, pal. The old lady don't like it, so I *especially* don't like it."

The volcano rumbled.

"See?" Heena said.

"That's hooey!" Wally Junior shouted. "It's bull hockey that pops has been feeding you gals to keep you out of his treasure! Treasure is for men, see! Women would only blow treasure on frilly junk instead of investing it in making more treasure!"

The volcano rumbled some more.

"I think you fellas better rethink this whole expedition," I said.

"Horse apples, chum!" Konrath said. "I radioed out to the ship. My men are already out there in the pearl beds. As far as I know, it's all good and legal. I bring attorneys with me everywhere I go, and they say we can take anything out of there, including every pearl we find."

"*Taboo!*" Heena shouted.

"Taboo!" the girls all shouted.

Louise, Judy and Irene came out with their beaux hot on their little tails. "What's happening? Why is Mondo angry?"

"Taboo!" Heena shouted, pointing at Konrath.

The admiral's helo turned on, and he hopped aboard, along with his aide. Tank appeared with the radio and handed the handset to Buzz.

"There's room for everyone in the landing craft coming ashore in twenty minutes," Buzz said. "Let's go."

"Go?" Dottie asked.

"Yes, my love. Go," he said taking her hands in his. "Let's get everyone on the boat. If Mondo doesn't destroy the island in his rage, anyone who wants to come back here may do so."

"Fair enough," Dottie said. "Let's go, girls."

Mondo burped and a glowing rock arced high up in the sky and came tumbling down and blew up the jeep. We all ducked.

"What about the XAD-53, sir?" Mitch asked, thumbing at it.

"Leave it behind. If the island blows, it can blow with it."

"Aye, sir!"

Louise scurried up on Mitch's back.

"Nothing's happening. It's just a little trembler," Konrath said. "A minor eruption."

"You're all heathens who believe in hogwash!" Wally Junior said. "You're all suckers!"

The lads came running up and asked if Konrath was all right.

Mondo rumbled ominously.

We all ran.

The Wrath of Mondo!

We neared the shore. The ground shook, knocking us all off our feet, and a massive projectile fired out of the mouth of the volcano. It roared like a V-2 rocket, leaving an ashen vapor trail behind it as it streaked out toward a hazy white ship silhouetted on the blue horizon.

"That's my ship," Konrath said, his mouth dropping open.

"Taboo," Heena said, picking herself up and wagging a finger at him. "Taboo!"

The projectile hit the freighter amidships and it immediately cracked in half.

"Now what do you think of Mondo, you pipsqueak?" O'Neill asked Wally Junior.

"That don't prove nothing," Wally Junior said, sneering at the much larger man. "You're a sucker. You're all suckers!"

The Navy landing craft was parked next to Konrath's much larger privately owned LST. "I'm going to go to the pearl beds and get my men. Then we'll head out to the fleet," Konrath said. "Who's with me?"

Both Wally's stepped aboard the LST. So did Elvgren.

The three newest employees of the Konrath Lines—Art, Les and Marty—hesitated. All three of them were still wearing their bespoke suits. They'd very clearly slept in them in the jungle.

"I'm frightened!" Marty admitted, winded, hands on knees.

"Get in the boat. *Now*," Konrath commanded, waving them onboard.

"Getting in the boat!" Marty said, and the other two followed behind.

Konrath hopped onboard and fired up the engine. "See you in the funny papers, chum!" he called out, waving. The big door slammed shut.

We got into the Navy landing craft, the door closing behind us, and the coxswain, dixie cup cocked jauntily upon his head, maneuvered it out to sea. He turned around and gawked at the beautiful island girls. A toothpick fell out of his mouth.

"Eyes on the road, buster," Dottie said.

And he turned back around.

The volcano was in full eruption now, spewing rocks, ash and vomiting lava down its sides. Smoke rose from where the village had been, and then came a strange green glow that I assumed came from the XAD-53's destruction.

As Old Man Konrath's boat bobbed toward the pearl beds, we were unsurprised by the projectile that landed squarely atop it, sinking it instantly.

"Daddy!" Irene wailed mournfully. Hondo carefully picked her up in his arms and held her, turning her face away from the scene of incredible destruction.

Epilogue: The War Against the Reds (and Professor Greenwood) Continues!

Dottie and Heena outrank me, but I have no problem with that. We're all in the Navy now. Have been for the past few years. Even the girls. Even our two Japanese compatriots, who were granted citizenship and inducted into the Navy by Ike himself.

Maybe I'm getting ahead of myself.

We live on Naval Base Foxtrot, an artificial island created by Professor Greenwood, who used radio waves and some other complicated gizmos to manipulate a fissure on the bottom of the ocean. The lava poured upward and he formed for himself an island lair, also known to the Navy as "Objective Alpha Mike Foxtrot" before we took it away from him. He escaped. He keeps escaping. He's good at it.

Anyway, I'm a warrant officer now, in charge of maintaining the base and the USS *Devil Ray*, our super secret speedboat. It has rockets on it and a nearly silent motor. A lot of my day is involved in keeping the 200 base workers happy. They're mostly civilians, and mostly unionized. I deal with a grievance or two a week. We have a fire department, security detail, public works, two galleys, and so on. Plus, there are some scientists here from the Office of Naval Research who study the girls' psychic link with the semi-active volcano that was created by Professor Greenwood when he made this place. We try to tell them about Maui (Mondo) Tiki, but they aren't having it.

I report to Lt. Dottie Pepper, the XO of UDT Six. Her husband, Lt. Cmdr. Buzz Pepper, is our CO. Master Chief Jack O'Neill completes our command triad as the senior enlisted leader.

Turned out that Toshiro's uncle was a karate master, so we brought him in to teach us all hand-to-hand fighting techniques. The girls picked up on it right away, especially Louise, Judy and Irene, who are all three petty officers now, and are the most important part of our infiltration team. For some reason, we run into a lot of pipes and air conditioning ductwork in our adventures, so those three gals come in mighty handy by being tiny, but deadly. Their wee hands are registered with the FBI as lethal weapons, I'm given to understand.

When we took this island, Louise crawled through the ductwork and was above Professor Greenwood in his boardroom (which is now subdivided into offices for our supply clerks). She pressed the button on her miniature wrist radio, and we were all privy to his plans. But Louise inhaled a little bit of dust and sneezed, and the professor's henchmen pulled her out of the vent and set her on the table in front of Greenwood. The professor shouted into the wrist radio, "We have her now!" and then he laughed quite a bit. Excessively, you might say.

"I hurt my ankle," Louise said, with a pout in her voice.

The henchmen all went, "Aww," because Louise is pretty darned adorable.

And that's when Irene, Hondo, Judy, Toshiro, Sandy, Master Chief, Ruby, Hiro and Mitch came busting in. Louise leapt up and joined in on the punching and kicking party, and almost tackled Professor Greenwood before he made it to his escape pod.

Just another day at the office, I guess.

We have a family dinner once a week—when we don't have a mission to perform, that is. We gather together on the beach, pile up wood for a bonfire, and listen to Hicks and Betty sing songs. Betty got hold of a Les Paul electric guitar at some point, and she can make that guitar flat out talk.

Gloria and Scrimshaw always make a new banner for the picnic. They run the base newspaper, which is done in the form of a weekly comic book, so everyone can keep up to date on the adventures of our team.

Tank, Elroy, Franny and Lizzie ride their surfboards until the sun goes down.

I see Hondo and Irene curled up together, looking out to sea. I see Mitch and Louise returning from a walk along the shoreline.

Heena is the chaplain for our base. She's a lieutenant in the chaplain corps, with her rank on one collar and a tiki idol (instead of a cross) on the other collar of her khakis. Before dinner, after being called to attention to evening colors by Dottie and after we salute the national ensign at the end of the day, Lt. Russo leads us all in prayer to Mondo (Maui) Tiki, and we thank him for the life he's granted us. He rumbles his pleasure.

We have two kids added to our extended family already. There's little Chester Nimitz O'Neill, who isn't all that little, come to think of it. Sandy chases him as Chester bulls around the beach like a fullback, and the Chief stands at his place near the fire grinning ear-to-ear.

And, of course, there's Heena's and my little girl,

Kohara, who stands next to me while her mother leads us in prayer. She has her mother's eyes, blue and green and filled with golden stars, and her mother's generous heart.

Thank you, Mondo!

UDT Six will be back in…

THE RED MARAUDERS AND THE SHARK TEMPLE OF BLOOD

www.ingramcontent.com/pod-product-compliance
Lightning Source LLC
Chambersburg PA
CBHW061550170626
46811CB00001B/156